Linc was nuzzling her neck, whispering

"Jude, Jude, my Jude."

But I'm not yours, she wanted to yell.

"Relax," he murmured.

"I *am* relaxed."

"You're not, but you will be," he assured her. He kissed her, nibbling seductively at her lips until her mouth opened of its own accord, allowing him access to gulp in her sweetness like a man finding an oasis after months in the desert. Little by little, he was relearning the contours of her body, and she felt herself responding to his will. But he was "someone else".

"Linc, it's well after midnight, shouldn't you get some sleep?"

"I can sleep later, right now I want to eat you," he declared. Her blood raced. She knew that whoever he was, whoever he had become, she needed him. But how could she feel like this when half her mind was shrieking that he was a stranger?

ELIZABETH OLDFIELD

beloved stranger

Harlequin Books

TORONTO • NEW YORK • LONDON
AMSTERDAM • PARIS • SYDNEY • HAMBURG
STOCKHOLM • ATHENS • TOKYO • MILAN

Harlequin Presents first edition December 1983
ISBN 0-373-10652-1

Original hardcover edition published in 1983
by Mills & Boon Limited

CHAPTER ONE

'HEY, Jude, what's the rush?'

The staccato march of high heels across the marbled mezzanine floor ceased abruptly. Snatching dark glasses from her nose, Judith Cassidy swung round, ash-blonde hair tumbling over one shoulder.

'Don't call me Jude.'

The young man's lower lip jutted sulkily. 'Linc does. Did.'

She frowned as the change of tense registered, but let it pass. *'Only* Linc,' she retorted.

He shrugged, smiling his disarming all-American-boy smile, and Judith relented. It was unfair to expect Wayne to bear the brunt of her mood; he wasn't responsible for the tension coiled around her temples like a wire tourniquet, twisting tighter and tighter as the days passed by.

'I'm sorry, I'm feeling rather uptight.'

'You are allowed to show your feelings, sugar. Yell blue murder or throw a fit,' he teased, his eyes gentle upon her.

'Public displays of the inner self are not my style, as you well know,' she replied, the sharpness of her tone signalling an end to the conversation.

She slipped the owl-framed sunglasses into her shoulder bag as they resumed their journey along the wide shopping arcade. Now the glare of the tropical sun and the sticky heat had been left behind, held at bay outside the sliding glass doors of the Sentosa Country Club. Here, cushioned in the air-conditioned coolness, was a different world—a world of restrained elegance. A world which pampered and indulged those inter-

5

national travellers able to afford the most luxurious hotel on the island of Penang. Here sweat wouldn't dare to trickle down between your shoulder-blades, Judith thought wryly, or mosquitoes whine in your ear. The contrast between the real world outside, with its sweltering *kampungs* teeming with Asian life, and the spacious manicured lifestyle provided for the tourists, always intrigued her.

'What's the rush?' Wayne Templeton repeated, lengthening his stride to keep pace with her hurrying steps. 'None of the stores are open yet.'

'Boutiques,' she grinned, recovering her usual poise. 'Boutiques sounds more up-market than stores.'

He smiled, catching her eye. 'Boutiques then, what the hell! With an up-market dame in charge of the antique section.'

'Thank you, kind sir,' she said lightly, enjoying the compliment and yet at the same time unsettled by it. Deliberately she turned from the intimate gaze of his grey eyes to scan the window displays—hand-tooled leather goods, sparkling diamonds, the latest in high fashion, wristwatches in stainless steel and gold. Discreet lettering on the shop doors revealed names of international repute—Lanvin, Girard-Perregaux, Van Cleef and Arpels, Gucci. Impressive neighbours for an ex-airline hostess from England, she admitted, but she was more than holding her own. Business was flourishing. As they turned the corner and the familiar double plateglass windows of Mandarin Antiques came into view, her blue eyes lit up. The sight of the gleaming Korean chests, the cabinets inlaid with mother-of-pearl, the Chinese pottery and the silverware imparted a comforting glow of satisfaction. Mandarin Antiques was her life now—it was all she had.

She searched in her bag for the keys. 'I like to be early. It's easier if I deal with the post and get any necessary telephoning out of the way before the first customers arrive.'

'Come on, Judith,' Wayne remonstrated, rubbing a hand across his wide jaw. 'Surely Rosiah can cope with a few tourists?'

A key was selected from the clutch on her ring. 'Rosiah's very efficient,' she agreed with reluctance.

'Be honest, she's totally reliable. You should delegate more.'

Her chin took on a stubborn slant. 'I prefer to speak to the customers myself. I know more about the history of the various pieces than Rosiah. After all, the shop . . .'

'The boutique,' he cut in, grinning.

'The boutique,' she adjusted, 'is my bread and butter.'

'And jam.'

'Yes, thank goodness. It's really taken off during the past six months.'

'You're turning out to be a very bright lady,' Wayne murmured close to her ear. 'Hard-working, intelligent, with a shrewd eye for a bargain, and in addition to all that with one helluva good figure.'

'I seem to remember you telling me I was a wacky dame,' she returned smartly, determined to keep the mood lighthearted. There was something in Wayne's attitude this morning which disturbed her, some shift of emotion she didn't feel prepared to analyse. He had always been open about his affection for her. There was a standing joke—he insisted that if he had met her first Linc would never have stood a chance. All in fun, of course, for Wayne, Linc's cousin, had been safely married to Esther for the past ten years. Judith frowned; safely was not the right word. Linc had hinted that Wayne had strayed from the straight and narrow on more than one occasion. She checked herself, refusing to think deeper. Now was not the time for

probing Wayne's feelings when it was all she could do
to cope with her own.

'You sure were one wacky dame *then*,' he drawled,
laughing.

The brief intensity in his eyes had vanished and she
relaxed. As they reached the door of the antique shop
she thrust the key into the lock. 'What do you mean—
then?' she asked. She bent down to release the bolt at
floor level, the creamy-white suede of her skirt
stretching across her hips, outlining the curves.

'Grr!' He gave a low growl and reached for her waist
as she straightened.

Judith stepped aside to avoid contact. 'You mean
before Linc disappeared, don't you?' she demanded.
She and Wayne had never pulled any punches between
them, and now was not the time to start. He had always
been honest and open with her, never avoiding the issue
like so many others.

'Mmm,' he agreed, nodding. 'When he was here he
ran the show. I guess you were content to sit back and
let it happen.' Wayne studied the gold lettering on the
door: J. Cassidy, Proprietor. 'He'd have one helluva
shock if he knew you'd become a business-woman and
a real successful one at that.'

'I wasn't helpless when he was here,' she protested.
'You have the wrong impression. I was an airline
stewardess for five years, I've always been capable.'

He gave a mocking bow of acquiescence. 'Okay,' he
smiled. 'I concede you have a high I.Q., it's just that it
wasn't so blatant before.'

Judith wrinkled her nose in exasperation. 'In all
fairness, I could never have taken over the shop without
Linc's assistance,' she admitted. 'Although he doesn't
know it, he provided the finance. Most of the cash came
from the sale of the Mercedes.'

She stood on tiptoe, fingers straining for the bolt at
the top of the door. Wayne watched, feasting on the

taut line of her body as she stretched, her heavy ash-blonde hair covering her shoulders, pale against the black silk of her blouse. With pert breasts, slender waist and shapely hips, she had all the right things in all the right places, he acknowledged for the thousandth time. Linc was a lucky devil.

He broke his reverie. 'Move over,' he ordered, striding forward to reach above her to release the bolt.

'What would I do without you?' she joked, but immediately regretted her words. She was almost within the circle of his arms, too close to the broad expanse of checkered shirtfront for comfort. Wayne had been so good to her, *for* her, but there were hints that his attitude was changing.

Judith sidestepped. A scatter of morning post lay on the marble floor. 'Actually I can manage extremely well on my own,' she added firmly, lifting the letters and catching the door wide. She marched inside, all too conscious of the fact that Wayne was following close behind. Reaching a wide, leather-topped desk, she scampered behind it and swivelled to confront him. 'It was very decent of you to come,' she began pedantically. 'And I really do appreciate it, but . . .'

A burst of laughter stopped her words.

'You sound so goddam English at times,' he chuckled, pushing the floppy fair hair from his brow. He paused to mimic her, abandoning his Californian drawl for a plummy English accent. 'I really do appreciate it.'

'But I *am* English,' she protested.

'You've been married to a . . . a Yank for almost two years,' he pointed out. 'I'd have expected some American twang to have infiltrated by now.'

'Well, it hasn't, and as Linc has been missing for the past twelve months you can hardly count that period as our married life.'

'*Almost* twelve months,' he interrupted, folding his arms and subjecting her to a penetrating scrutiny.

Judith turned away, leafing through the envelopes in her hand. There was no need to spell it out. She knew only too well how many months, how many weeks, how many days, it was since Linc had been taken hostage. Indeed, one endless evening when she had been alone at the bungalow she had taken out her pocket calculator and morbidly totted up how many hours and minutes it had been since she had last seen him, last exchanged a loving intimate glance, last felt his mouth on hers, last thrown herself into his arms. The total had been alarming and once again she had sobbed herself to sleep.

She slid a tapered finger beneath the flap of an envelope, slowly tearing it open. 'There was no need for you to come this morning,' she persisted, snapping the trapdoor shut on her troubled thoughts.

Wayne lolled against the side of the desk. 'I must hand it to you, sugar, that British stiff upper lip of yours is working overtime these days. Again and again I reckon you're about to give in and have a damn good cry, then the shutters roll down and you're brisk and businesslike. The ice maiden.'

Avoiding his eyes, she looked beyond his shoulder to a glossy poster on the far wall. 'Penang, Pearl of the Orient' it announced, picturing lush palms, a silver-white strip of sand and an azure sea stretching out to the horizon beneath a cloudless sky. The beach could be anywhere, for the island was fringed with idyllic coves, but she knew exactly where the photograph had been taken—Monkey Bay. A remote spot which she and Linc had discovered when they had been out sailing one weekend. They had found a shady clearing among the palm trees, and drunk wine, and made long lazy love. . . . She curled her fingers, the nails biting into her hands. 'I've told you before, I don't believe in letting it all hang out in public,' she rejoined tartly. 'Like some people.'

'Like Americans?' he queried, the corner of his mouth lifting in amusement.

'Perhaps in general Americans are more ... more extrovert than the British,' she admitted. 'Actually I was thinking of Magda, not that she's your typical American.'

Her mother-in-law possessed a flamboyant range of emotions from plunging despair to delirious joy, emotions which Judith had found embarrassing on many occasions, for Magda believed in telling the world exactly how she felt, and in dramatic detail. In the early days when her son had first been taken hostage, Magda had visited Penang, where she had proceeded to weep tragically on every available male shoulder, though never quite enough to loosen the adhesive on her false eyelashes. Not for her the unflattering puffiness of uncontrolled tears; instead she had clasped her hands in a series of pathetic gestures which Judith had unkindly attributed to some ancient B movie.

'My son, my devoted son,' Magda had blubbered, explaining in haste that he had been born when she was merely a girl. 'Poor me, what a struggle life has been! First my husband snatched from me by the hand of fate and now to lose my only child! We had a special relationship, we were so close.'

Judith had been forced to bite back a sharp denial at this distortion of the truth. Linc had left home as a teenager nearly twenty years before and only visited his mother under duress. It was his highly developed sense of duty which prompted him to respond to her shrill and mindless demands. Little-girl-lost was the role she had elected to play, a role Judith considered curious for a woman in her mid-fifties, but apparently it had always been so. Magda would never change. Invariably Linc vowed that *next* time he would refuse to answer his mother's cries for attention, but he never did.

He had no illusions. Magda's urge for his presence

always erupted when some man friend had grown
weary of her high-voltage posturing and she had not yet
found a replacement. Her son was the one steady male
in her life, he couldn't get away. Or more to the point,
Judith amended, a deep-seated loyalty bound him to
her. When a gap appeared in Magda's life she
bombarded him with letters and phone calls no matter
where he was, and should there be no immediate
response she would arrive on his doorstep, without
notice, shrieking for an audience.

Wayne's mouth curved into a wide grin. 'Magda gets
through more crises in a day than most folk meet in a
lifetime. Linc always maintained his father died of
nervous exhaustion! She's a real pain in the . . .' His
voice trailed off. 'Dad has no time for her, you'd never
imagine they were brother and sister. He plays
everything close to his chest, while Aunt Magda . . .
When she starts out on those stories of hers, hinting the
family are descended from wealthy White Russian
princes, well, Dad really hits the roof! Magda's a great
gal for romancing. She should have been an actress.' He
shook his head in amused disbelief. 'Linc would play
hell if he could hear the embarrassing way she
buttonholes complete strangers and embroiders the
facts. She alters her version of his disappearance,
depending on who's listening. I've even heard her
suggest that Linc's a secret agent with a direct line to
the President!' He gave a low whistle. 'Thank goodness
he's a competent guy of thirty-five with his feet firmly
planted on the ground. All his life she's tried to make
him responsible for her, even from a distance.'

Judith shrugged helplessly. 'Emotionally she's never
let go. You would think he was the parent and she was
the child. He's very patient with her.'

'Too patient! I'd have shown her the door long ago.'

'He can't do that,' she protested. 'He is her only
child.'

'She demands too much.'

A giggle rose in her throat. 'He really spoiled her plans when he committed the mortal sin of marrying an ordinary English girl!'

Wayne laughed. 'You fluffed your lines there, sugar. You should have given yourself a title to keep her happy.'

'I bet she's spread the word back home that I'm on intimate terms with dukes and duchesses,' she chuckled. 'You know what she was like at our wedding, desperate to discover links between my family and the aristocracy.'

'But there's no girls as cute as the Californian girls,' Wayne chanted in a fair imitation of his aunt's drawl. 'She wasn't at all keen on the prospect of Linc getting married, but if he did she always hoped it would be to that Suzanne, the millionaire's daughter he knew in Palm Beach. She had it mapped out how he would live in a gigantic villa on the coast with a nearby apartment laid on for her.' He shuddered. 'A fate worse than death.'

Wayne's view of Magda ran on parallel lines to her son's. The two men had grown up together in Los Angeles, playing in the same neighbourhood, attending the same college. When Linc had enlisted in the Air Force Wayne had not been far behind, and later they had both become pilots for a commercial airline. Three years ago Wayne had eagerly accepted a partnership when Linc had set up a private helicopter company in Penang.

'Living in the same State as Magda would be sheer unadulterated hell,' Judith declared, her mouth twitching with laughter. 'Even the same country would be dicey, she'd never leave you alone.'

'Doesn't Linc know it! He cut loose the minute he possibly could. Why do you suppose he decided to become a pilot? So that he could soar off into the wide blue yonder and leave Magda's yakking far behind.'

She giggled. 'I do enjoy talking with you, Wayne. You lift my spirits, you're a kind of therapy.' The letter fluttered on to the desk and she walked round to him, resting cool fingers on his wrist. 'Everyone else handles me with kid gloves. They either avoid raising the subject of Linc entirely or are so ... so solicitous it makes me want to cringe. People don't seem to know how to react, how to comfort me. To be fair, I suppose there's not much comfort to give to a woman whose husband has been held hostage for so long.' Her fingers tightened involuntarily. 'You bring Linc into sharper focus. It's as though he's here and now when I'm talking to you.' She gave a wisp of a smile. 'Thank you.'

'But he isn't here and now, sugar.' Wayne covered her hand with his, and as stricken blue eyes were raised he glimpsed the desolation so carefully controlled. 'I'm sorry, but it's time you faced facts. Linc has been missing for almost twelve months with no news whatsoever. You'll have to accept the possibility he might never return.'

She clamped her eyelids tight shut. 'No,' she muttered. 'No, no, not yet.'

'In five days' time he'll have been gone twelve full months. We agreed initially we'd give it a year before reaching any conclusions.'

'*You* said a year.'

He sighed. 'I know it's harsh, Judith, but you can't go on forever hoping he'll come back. Linc wouldn't want you to exist like this for the rest of your days.'

'Like what?' she demanded wildly.

'Like some dedicated spinster.' His eyes travelled across the rich display of furniture and ornaments. 'There's more to life than running an antique shop in a hotel shopping arcade. You're far too young and pretty to cut yourself off forever from the idea of a husband and family.'

'I have a husband,' she retorted. Her voice fell away. 'And I almost had a family.'

'When you miscarried it was a blessing in disguise,' Wayne said with uncharacteristic bluntness. He took hold of her elbow, but when she tried to twist away his grip was firm. 'Face up to it. If the baby had lived you would never have been in a position to run a business. And if you had had a child your parents, and Magda, would have applied pressure on you to leave Penang. It's only because Esther and I are here that they have accepted the situation.' He gave her a little shake. 'Though why the hell you insist on living alone at the bungalow defeats me. You'd be far better off here in the hotel. Mr Cheng said you could move in any time you wanted.'

'Don't try and run my life for me,' she threatened. 'I'm not alone at the bungalow, Ah Fong comes in to sleep most nights. And as far as staying in Penang is concerned, well ...' She began to stumble over the words. 'At least I'm close to Linc ge—geographically. I'll be here when he returns.' She took a deep breath. 'I intend to remain here for ever.'

With a sinking feeling she realised that Wayne's attitude was changing in more ways than one. It was the first time he had been so forthright about the baby, and it hurt. She had not been aware of her pregnancy when Linc had been taken hostage. Two months later she had lost the child and had been too distraught to assess coldbloodedly whether it was for good or ill. Linc's child would have been a tangible reminder of him, but fate had stepped in. After the initial torment when her grief had swamped her, she had reached a decision—the only way to cope was to find an alternative outlet for her emotions. Self-indulgent despair was counterproductive, there was no point in brooding. Mandarin Antiques had cropped up, and she regarded it as a godsend. She swallowed to ease an

agonising lump in her throat. Surely she should be
hardened to the loss of the baby and Linc's absence by
now, but instead she seemed to be growing more
vulnerable.

'Next week I'll reassess the situation,' she promised,
forcing a half-hearted smile. 'At least allow me a full
year, don't push.'

'I'm not pushing,' he assured her. 'It would be
different if there had been a ransom note, if not for
Linc at least for Kee-Ann. As soon as the kidnappers
discovered she was the daughter of the millionaire, Mr
Cheng Boon Seng, you'd have imagined they would have
zoomed in on the money angle.'

'So you think there's . . .' her voice cracked. 'There's
no hope?' She couldn't bring herself to say what she
feared, that Linc was dead. The idea certainly wasn't
new; the prospect tormented her, swirling around and
around in her head as she lay alone in bed at night.

'I honestly don't know. Mr Cheng has had the jungle
border of Malaysia and Thailand combed as thoroughly
as is humanly possible. He's spared no expense. But it's
a vast area. Searching for a small group of Communist
insurgents is like finding a needle in a haystack.' He
eased his grip on her elbow. 'Have you heard anything
more from the U.S. Consul?'

As he dropped his hand Judith took a step
backwards. It had been a mistake to allow Wayne to
touch her; she had seen his eyes darkening, sensed that
his blood pressure was rising.

'There's nothing fresh. The man from the Consulate
is kind and understanding, but he knows no more than
we do, only that Linc and Kee-Ann were abducted a
few miles north of the border into Thailand by a small
band of terrorists.'

Wayne's grey eyes followed her as she walked back
around the desk to sit down. Lifting the discarded
letter, she pretended to study it. Don't look at me like

that, she implored silently. You're an attractive man and I'm fond of you, you've been as close as a brother to me, but that's all. When Linc had first disappeared she had fled into Wayne's arms for comfort, never thinking of him as anything but her husband's cousin, a close friend, yet now . . .

Unseeingly she stared at the black print. She had been grateful for his unstinting care and consideration. Yet, on second thoughts, hadn't she also relished the feel of his arms around her, the physical maleness of him at her side? Yes, she had. It was a brutally honest admission, the first time she had viewed their relationship from that angle. Twelve months was too long to go without touching, caressing, loving. She was lonely. Linc, she sobbed inwardly, come home soon, my darling.

She shook her head, bringing her thoughts back to a less emotional level. 'Mr Cheng came to see me yesterday. He's full of confidence that Linc and Kee-Ann will soon be discovered in good health. He appears to have the utmost faith in Linc's ability to squeeze out of tight corners.'

'So do I,' Wayne chimed, falling in chameleon-like with her comment. 'Cool calm control, all low-key stuff, that's our boy. After a lifetime coping with Magda, a band of Communists must be easy meat.'

Her tension began to fade. Optimism was what she required, there was no point being negative. Eventually she would face up to the worst, but not yet. Matters could ride until next week. 'How's Esther?' she asked, pinning on a bright smile.

'Obsessed with Robbie as usual,' he replied drily. 'Robbie's teething problems, Robbie's diaper rash, Robbie's mental and physical development *ad nauseam*. You'd think he was the first infant who ever drew breath.'

Judith swallowed down a smile at his grimace of wry

disgust. 'He is your son and heir, and you were married years and years before you produced him. Esther was desperate to have a child; it's obvious she's bound to be interested in him.'

'Interested! she's fanatical. I suggested we leave him with the *amah* and grab a weekend alone in Singapore, but she wouldn't hear of it. Ever since he was born six months ago she's been cooped up in the house, you'd imagine she would be desperate for freedom.' He snorted. 'And now her latest idea is that we start trying again for a second child.' His mouth thinned. 'No way.'

The severity of his look took her by surprise. 'Why not?'

'Because I don't reckon the odds are favourable for a marriage where the wife is obsessed with her offspring.'

Judith stared at him in alarm. 'And what exactly does that mean?'

'Nothing,' he bit out. 'But it doesn't do much for a guy's self-esteem if he's only expected to make love purely to produce a child. It was bad enough before we had Robbie, performing to order on the right day, at the right time. I'm sure as hell not going through that charade again. If all she wants is a father for her children, she can look elsewhere.'

'Don't worry, Esther's only passing through a phase,' she said soothingly, trying to stem her amusement at the image of 'performing to order' as he had phrased it so succinctly. 'She'll soon realise the sun doesn't rise and set over Robbie.'

'Will she?' he sulked, rubbing his thigh against the corner of the desk.

Wayne was overreacting, she decided. Esther was a homely girl whose one aim was to rear a brood of children and have a happy family life. It didn't seem too much to ask.

'Look, why don't the three of you come and spend this weekend with me at the bungalow?' she suggested. 'I'll be at the shop in the mornings, but I can arrange to have the afternoons free. As you said, it'll do me good to delegate for a change, and the trip up here will give Esther a break. I know it's still Penang, but it is a different part of the island. You can use the pool here too, Mr Cheng allows us free access.'

'I'll try and persuade her. I suppose there's a chance she might agree to a short excursion with the boy wonder,' Wayne said cryptically. He glanced at his watch. 'I'd better go upstairs and see if Mr Cheng is ready. I'm ferrying him to the airport, then we're flying south to Singapore.'

Mr Cheng Boon Seng, a longstanding friend of Linc's, had provided some of the capital for the helicopter company, on the understanding that he and his family had first call on their services. The arrangement worked well. With business interests throughout South-East Asia, the energetic Mr Cheng travelled virtually non-stop. When he had taken up residence in the penthouse atop the Sentosa Country Club, one of his many property investments, hangars and a helicopter pad had been erected adjacent to the grounds. Linc and Judith had rented a bungalow within easy reach of the hotel in the north of the island, while Wayne had taken a house alongside Bayan Lepas Airport in the south, an hour's drive away.

It had been routine for Linc to take Mr Cheng to the airport by helicopter, where they transferred to one of the executive planes for journeys further afield. In those days Wayne had dealt with the tourist side of the business, flying holiday-makers to offshore islands or on the short hop to Butterworth on mainland Malaysia. Within months the company had gained a name for reliability—Linc being a stickler for regular and expert servicing of the aircraft and good customer relations.

With a flourish Judith produced a spare key from her bag. 'Here you are, let yourselves in. Come any time Saturday, and if I'm not at the bungalow I'll be here.'

'Thanks,' Wayne said, pocketing it.

'Are you continuing to have a surplus of passengers for the planes?' she asked, moving around the shop, flicking on switches of table lamps and wall lights until the room was suffused with a soft golden glow.

'More than we can deal with,' he confirmed.

'Then why don't you . . .'

'Expand?' he filled in with a grin. 'I'm not your husband you know, always stretching further. I'd be happy to cruise along as we are now. However, Mr Cheng feels we must develop, so I'm going across to Sabah with him after Singapore. There's some guy there who wants to offload a couple of virtually brand-new Fokkers. We're going to give them the once-over.'

'Don't drag your feet,' she said smartly.

He pulled a face. 'I used to imagine that only Linc lived life twice as fast as everyone else, but now I suspect you're following suit.' He scratched the wide-angled jaw. 'You've changed, sugar. Linc's going to have a helluva lot to handle when . . .' he hesitated. '*If* he comes home.'

The ashen hair blinkered her expression as she bent her head to the letters. Resolutely she ignored the message he was giving her. When? If? Linc had to come home, he *had* to.

I must make Wayne understand his allegiance is to Esther, not to me, Judith determined as he sloped amiably away down the arcade. She scribbled a note in the margin of one of the letters and sat back, tossing the fall of thick hair over her shoulder. She must warn him off, but how could she do so without hurting him?

He had arrived at the bungalow that morning as she was eating breakfast, saying he knew her car was in for servicing and he would drive her to the hotel. It was a kind gesture, but unnecessary. Taxis were continually passing on the road outside the bungalow on their way

to and from the Sentosa Country Club, and if, for some
reason, no taxi had appeared, she could have walked.
True, she would have arrived hot and sticky, for it was
midsummer, humidity was high and the tropical sun
merciless even in the morning, but she would have soon
recovered.

Silently she vowed that at the first opportunity she
would do some straight talking. She would make it
plain he must devote his spare time to his wife, not to
her. A delicate turn of phrase would be needed to reject
his attentions after she had welcomed them so readily.
In retrospect she had been a trifle naïve, allowing him
to come so close. She gnawed unhappily at her lip. If
her senses were properly attuned, he was edging them
into an altogether different ballgame—a ballgame
which could only spell disaster. But he was wrong if he
imagined she would ever do anything to upset his
relationship with Esther, even if their marriage was
passing through a shaky patch. They had both
welcomed her into the family, supporting her without
reservation when Magda's chagrin at Linc's choice of
bride, or even a bride at all, had been only too flagrant.
Since Robbie's birth Judith hadn't seen so much of Esther,
but that was understandable. When Linc had been
around they had often made up a foursome, and
enjoyed an easy friendship which was precious to her.
She mustn't shatter that friendship. Reflectively she
sucked at the end of her pen. If only Wayne wasn't so
attentive, if only Linc had not been captured. Linc,
beloved Linc, her thoughts always circled back to the
original starting point—to Linc.

How well she remembered the devastating impact of
their first meeting. She and Teresa, another air hostess,
had arrived at their usual stopover hotel in Singapore
after a long flight, only to be told there had been
double-booking.

'No room at the inn,' Teresa had grumbled, but then

her gloom had lifted when she discovered they were being redirected to the Merlimau. 'Now that's what I call a hotel,' she had crowed.

The Merlimau was not normally used by British flight crews, being higher priced than most. Set like an expensive jewel amidst tropical gardens, it dripped affluence, and as they entered the chandeliered lobby Teresa had gripped Judith's arm.

'All this and American pilots, too,' she had giggled, pretending to swoon. 'Don't look now, but there's the most dishy-looking hunk at reception.' She had smoothed down the skirt of her smart navy suit and readjusted the bowler atop her dark curls.

Just being told not to look had been enough to whet Judith's appetite, and as she walked across the acres of lobby, her eyes followed Teresa's to a tall lean-hipped man lounging against the counter. Like her, he was in uniform, a peaked cap with gold braid beside his elbow. His gaze flicked over Teresa, dismissing her, but when it reached Judith the brown eyes stopped, locking with hers. Everything whirred to a halt. Although the Chinese receptionist was still talking to him, he swivelled to get a better look. Demanding his attention, the receptionist leant forward and in a moment of irritation he turned, sending his cap skimming across the marble floor to land at Judith's feet. Panther-like he leapt to retrieve it and somehow they collided, banging their heads. They straightened up, surveying each other.

'I'm sorry,' he said, smiling at her, rubbing his brow. His eyes were nutbrown, flecked with tiny yellow lights, she realised, warm eyes, crinkly lines at the corners.

'Did I hurt you?' he asked.

'No,' she said, grinning back.

His hair was thick, brownly glossy like autumn chestnuts. He looked a hairy kind of man. There was a smattering of dark hair on the back of his hands, and she wondered if his arms were hairy, and his chest, and his back? Hairy men turned her on.

'Your hat's crooked,' he said, his smile spreading wider. His face was tanned, his teeth white and even.

'Is it?' Judith raised a vague hand. There were creases which dimpled in his cheeks when he smiled.

'Here, let me help,' he said decisively. He thrust his own cap between his knees and raised both hands to her bowler, straightening it. Obediently she stood waiting until he was satisfied. He leant back. 'Beautiful,' he declared, and she knew he didn't mean the bowler. He put his cap on to the back of his head and kept on smiling. Judith smiled too, never wanting to stop.

'I'm trying to think of some witty way to ask you to have dinner with me this evening,' he told her. 'But I'm fresh out of ideas.'

'I do prefer to be picked up with style,' she teased, finding her tongue at last. Out of the corner of her eye she could see Teresa hovering impatiently. Let her wait, she thought. Let the receptionist wait, let everyone wait.

'Oh hell, suppose we pretend I'm concussed for now?' he grinned. 'I'll meet you here in the lobby at eight and in the meantime I'll have my scriptwriters come up with some devastating lines. Then we can start all over again.'

'And I'll think how brilliant you are?'

'You'll be so damn impressed,' he assured her, laughing.

Judith felt warm and happy inside.

'It's the bowler,' he said, making no move to leave her and return to the reception desk where the girl was frowning at him. 'I've always preferred macho women.'

'Do you want to feel my muscles?' she flirted, holding up an arm and flexing it.

'Oh honey, yes please.' He was smiling that gorgeous smile again. 'What's your name, apart from Miss Universe, that is?'

'Judith.'

'Jude,' he grinned.

She twitched a shoulder. 'Okay,' she agreed. In the past she had never cared for her name to be shortened, but when this tall rangy American purred 'Jude' it suddenly sounded exactly right. Must be something to do with his voice, she thought. He had a smooth low tone, rife with sensuality. Beneath the immaculate uniform was a muscled physique which was making her heart flutter. He was a vibrant, sexy animal, improbably disguised as a run-of-the-mill airline pilot. A man who spent his days weighed down with the responsibility of conveying hundreds of people from A to B, their lives in his hands. He had large hands, long tanned fingers with dark hairs on the knuckles, hands which she suspected knew exactly how to do what needed to be done. . . .

'I'm Lincoln Cassidy, Linc, in case you're interested.'

'I am,' she said. Oh brother, I *am*, she decided gleefully.

'Excuse me, sir.' The receptionist's patience was fast running out.

Lincoln Cassidy gave a wry smile. 'See you at eight, Jude.'

From that day on he had been the mainspring of her life.

'Love at first sight,' he had pronounced later.

'Lust at first sight,' she had teased, digging him in the ribs.

'Let's settle for both.'

They had.

Disconsolately Judith spun the pencil between her fingers.

'Mornin', missie.' Ah Fong, a butterball of a woman scarcely five feet tall, had waddled into the shop in her usual working garb of bright crimson tunic and loose black trousers. Her flipflop sandals smacked across the floor. 'Any news Mr Linc?' she asked.

Judith shook her head. 'No news.'

'Him still with guerillas. No news good news, I unnerstan'', the Chinese woman rattled off as she made for the cupboard where dusters and polish were kept. Judith suppressed a smile. Ah Fong, her *amah*, finished off every other sentence with 'I unnerstan'', though it was meaningless. Having spent all her life in Penang, her fractured English had been gleaned from the variety of expatriate families for whom she had worked over the years. Her pronunciation was excruciating. For weeks Judith had struggled to make sense of the simplest announcements, and even now it was debatable whether Ah Fong actually said 'guerillas' and if she did, did she know what it meant? There was a suspicion she believed Linc was holed up in the jungle with a band of monkeys.

'I go Snake Temple today,' she declared, wafting her feather duster across a display of blue and white vases.

'Thank you,' Judith replied politely.

Only days after Linc had disappeared Ah Fong had announced her intention of visiting the temple to ask her oriental gods to release him.

'She's going to make an offering,' Judith had told Wayne, her eyes stretched in awe.

He had been matter of fact. 'It won't be a sacrificial goat,' he had jeered. 'She'll stick a couple of mandarin oranges on to the altar for five minutes, say her prayers, then slip the oranges back into her shopping bag and take them home for her family. The Chinese are a practical race.'

'I still think it's very kind,' she had protested, hurt by his scepticism.

'I bet it doesn't work,' he had rejoined flatly.

So far, it hadn't.

'I go bungalow later, wash floors,' Ah Fong

continued, prattling on about her plans for the day while Judith lent half an ear. Every morning when the *amah* came in to clean the shop, she listed her proposed timetable in her pidgin English. Judith was always content to abide by her decisions. Ah Fong divided her time between the shop and the bungalow, with frequent trips down the road to the wooden house in the *kampung* where she supervised the lives of her taxi-driver husband, numerous offspring, sons and daughters-in-law, grandchildren and assorted cousins. Deciphering precise relationships was out of the question, for Ah Fong had blood and adopted relatives all over Penang, and was able to produce a nephew capable of disposing of a troublesome nest of hornets, or a daughter who was a dedicated seamstress, at a moment's notice.

When she had finished her dusting she squatted down on her haunches, vigorously applying polish to the brass fittings of a rosewood chest. Judith gave a smile of gratitude at the sleek black head, the hair combed back into a tight bun at the nape of her neck. Ah Fong was a kindly soul. No matter how pressing the demands of her large family, she reliably returned to the bungalow in the late evening to spend the night in her little room beyond the kitchen. She had never been asked to do this, but insisted it was 'bad missie be alone'. Steadfastly she refused to accept that the bungalow was secure, with strong iron grilles at the windows, and that Judith was not afraid. It was only on special occasions, such as Chinese New Year or family celebrations, that she could be persuaded to sleep at home. Judith often wondered what Ah Fong's husband thought of the arrangement. She couldn't imagine Linc being so amenable. He had always complained when he had been forced to spend even one night away from home on business. Linc, darling Linc, her thoughts were back with him again.

A soft breath of exasperation escaped her. Her guard was slipping, for usually when she was at the shop she was able to set her worries aside. She could feel the tension mounting within her as the time approached when he would have been gone a full year. What a dreadful anniversary, if that was what it could be called. Previously anniversaries had always spelled happiness, but now . . .

Her mind drifted to their first anniversary, how happy they had been. Linc had taken a day off work, deserting Mr Cheng, and they had sailed to Monkey Bay, just the two of them. It had been a special day, full of magic. He had lifted her, laughing, out of the dinghy into his arms and carried her through the crystal-clear shallows and up the wide beach. Then he had stretched out beside her on a towel beneath the palm trees and kissed away her tiny white crochet bikini and . . .

'Eh, missie, eh?' Ah Fong was saying loudly in her high-pitched oriental voice.

Judith blinked. 'Sorry?'

'I come late bungalow tonight, missie. Mimi got plenty people, me make *makan*.'

Mimi was one of Ah Fong's grown-up daughters. She had married a restaurant owner and called on her mother from time to time to help in the kitchens when a particularly large booking was arranged.

'That's fine. I'm perfectly safe. I might be late home myself this evening, but you have a key. Come whenever you're ready.'

'I unnerstan',' Ah Fong said glibly over her shoulder.

A smiling Malay girl in her early twenties hurried in through the open door. 'Good morning, Mrs Cassidy.'

' 'Morning, Rosiah,' Judith returned as she walked across to a filing cabinet hidden behind a lacquered chest of drawers.

The girl followed her. 'Any news of . . .'

Automatically Judith held her breath, waiting. Tension tap-danced along her nerves. She had the reply off pat and was therefore thrown off balance when Rosiah continued, 'of the consignment of brassware from Seoul?'

She gave a hiss of relief. Momentarily she had forgotten that her assistant was one of the people who avoided all mention of Linc and his predicament. She didn't know why. Perhaps the brown-skinned girl was worried her employer might break down in public, but she never had—Judith squared her shoulders—and never would.

'There's a copy bill of lading in the post. The boat should have arrived at George Town two days ago.' She pulled a folder from the drawer. 'Will you be okay if I leave you alone in the shop this afternoon? I'd like to go to the docks and confirm that everything is organised for an early delivery, then I'll motor on to see Mr Lim at Gertak Sanggul. I hear he's closing down and has a collection of pewter he wants to sell.' She grinned. 'I might pick up a bargain.'

'I never thought a European would be a match for a Chinese merchant,' Rosiah teased, her smile flashing white in the sultry complexion. 'But you are able to twist them around your little finger.'

Judith laughed. 'Perhaps it's beginner's luck.'

When she and Linc were newly married the bungalow had been her main interest. Shortly after their first meeting in Singapore he had resigned from the commercial airline, and by the time they were married the helicopter company in Penang had been well and truly launched. While he spent his days flying across the wide blue tropical skies, she happily devoted her time to furnishing their home. Judith had always been a collector, and when she settled in the Far East a whole new world of delicious treasures opened up. Linc was forever dragging her away from shabby old shops crowded with tantalising heaps of desks and chairs which she itched to restore to their former glory. He would stand by her side, arms patiently folded, a grin tugging at the corner of his mouth as she haggled with impassive Asians.

It was during her search for interesting local pieces to decorate the airy rooms that she had first walked through the doors of Mandarin Antiques and met Audrey, who was the owner. When the bungalow was furnished to her satisfaction, and within their budget, she was at a loss.

'Why don't you come in and give me a hand?' Audrey had suggested, for they were friends by now, and Judith had been off like a shot, working in the shop several afternoons a week.

Linc had viewed the development with wry satisfaction.

'It'll give those rich old roués something decorative to goggle at while their blue-rinsed wives are buying up souvenirs,' he said, tongue-in-cheek, as they lay sunbathing on the patio.

'This is for real, Lincoln Cassidy,' she had protested, kneeling up to straddle him. She pummelled his furry chest in mock indignation. 'I'm serious about antiques. One day I shall run a business of my own.'

He had caught hold of her arms and pulled her down on top of him. 'Perhaps later,' he'd said, kissing her ear. 'Right now, lady, your role in life is ministering to my needs.'

'And they are?' she had enquired, clinging to him, dreamily enjoying the masculine force of his body against hers.

His large hands had slid down across her shoulder-blades, her waist, to her hips. 'Don't tell me you don't know,' he had murmured, spreading his tanned fingers and grinding her against his thighs.

'I have a vague idea,' she had confessed as he began

to devour her, one degree at a time, loving her with such potency that within seconds she was at his mercy, limp and liquid in his arms.

After he had disappeared she had rushed to Mandarin Antiques every day. It was a bolt-hole. Only her miscarriage had broken the pattern, but she had returned to the shop within a week of her discharge from hospital.

'Are you sure you're well enough to be here?' Audrey had asked, scanning her friend's pale face.

Intensity burned deep in her blue eyes. 'I need to come. It's the only thing that keeps me going.'

One morning Audrey had arrived with the shock announcement that her husband, an expatriate business man, was being transferred to Hong Kong.

'I'll buy the stock and take over the lease,' Judith had said impulsively. She had cast around in her mind for ways of raising the necessary finance. 'We have some money in the bank, and I'll sell the Mercedes. I never did enjoy driving it, anyway. It's much too unwieldy and it drinks petrol. I'll buy myself something smaller.'

'Watch you don't put that into a drain,' Audrey had teased.

Once, in the first days of her marriage, Judith had been parking the large Mercedes and had inadvertently backed it over one of the storm drains which laced the streets of George Town, the capital of Penang. Fortunately, although deep, the drain was narrow. One wheel of the car became lodged and she had been forced to beg help from passers-by. Over a dozen sinewy Malays and Chinese had come to her aid and pushed the heavy vehicle free. Linc had greeted news of the escapade with a patronising air. It amused him and he never lost an opportunity of resurrecting the details, much to her fury. The error strengthened his deep-rooted belief that women always needed men to help them out of awkward situations. Judith's blood had boiled at the unspoken insinuation; then she had realised he had spent years taking charge of his mother's mindless foibles. It was no wonder he believed in male supremacy.

He would think differently now. Coming back to the present, she shone a satisfied beam of approval around the shop. This was her success, hers alone; even Wayne had contributed little to Mandarin Antiques, for she had refused to allow him to become involved, jealously keeping that part of her life to herself.

There was the tread of feet along the arcade, customers were arriving, the business day was starting. As a quartet of holidaymakers surged through the door she walked forward, a welcoming smile on her lips.

'Say, aren't those called Mandarin sleeves?' one of the women was asking, pointing to a display of embroidered squares, and Judith began to explain their history.

CHAPTER TWO

THERE was a steady flow of customers all morning, and the cash register rang with cheerful regularity. The afternoon had stretched to four o'clock by the time Judith was free to depart for the docks. Issuing instructions to Rosiah to close at six prompt, she strode away into the corridor. At one time she had considered staying open later in the evening, but now she was relieved she hadn't, enough was enough—even her enthusiasm had its limits. As she walked along, her bag swinging on her shoulder, she eyed the shop next door which stocked long-playing records and pirated cassette tapes. Large red notices proclaimed 'Closing Down Sale' and 'Everything Must Go'. The location was all wrong, Judith diagnosed, making for the staircase. Wealthy middle-aged jet-setters weren't interested in three-*ringgit* dollops of pop music. Trade would be far more brisk on a busy city street where young passers-by would be tempted in by the blare of the music and the prospect of bargain tapes.

She hailed a taxi outside the hotel and travelled the short distance to the garage to collect her car. Clean and shining, it had been freshly polished in addition to being serviced. Waving her thanks to the mechanic, she pulled out on to the road, winding the windows down wide to allow the balmy breeze to circulate. A temperature in the low nineties soon had damp wisps of hair clinging to her cheeks, and her blouse was sticking to her back when, half an hour later, she arrived at George Town docks. After making a few enquiries she located the man in charge of unloading, who assured her the cargo from Korea would be released and delivered to her in two days' time. Her eyes brightened at the prospect of exploring her purchases, and she was humming to herself as she returned to the car.

Nature's artist was daubing the sky with sunset shades of lemon and vermilion as Judith drove south towards Gertak Sanggul. Mr Lim had been one of Linc's passengers, flying regularly to Kuala Lumpur, and he and his wife greeted her eagerly, pressing her to stay for dinner and asking for the latest news of her husband. She hid behind an automatic response, relieved when the subject was played out and the conversation could be steered towards the pewterware.

There were stars shining in the velvet blackness of the night when she swung the small car into the drive of the bungalow. Climbing out, she stretched tiredly. It had been a long day, but a satisfying one. Mr Lim had settled for a reasonable price which kept them both happy. He had promised to deliver the pewter first thing in the morning and had also agreed to throw in some old bric-a-brac for free. She couldn't wait to get her hands on it, for she lived in the hope of discovering a valuable heirloom among the so-called trash. Yawning tiredly, she padded across the terrazzo-tiled living-room towards the bedroom. Perhaps tonight she would sleep; she hoped so, for sleep was proving to be an elusive commodity. The sudden jangle of the telephone in the stillness made her jump, and she laughed wryly at herself. Her nerves were becoming not only frayed, but downright unravelled.

'Hello?'

'Mrs Cassidy? It's Doug Reidman here from the U.S. Consulate.'

With a zing she was wide awake, standing to attention, her senses alerted to red for danger, her veins pulsating with expectation, with fear. It must be an emergency for the Consulate to ring at this time of night. She gripped the edge of the telephone table, her knuckles white with worry.

'Mrs Cassidy? Mrs Cassidy? Are you there?' he asked when she made no sound.

Her vocal cords appeared to have perished. 'I'm here,' she croaked at last, clearing her throat. How could she speak coherently when her heart was bouncing about in her breast like a rubber ball, sending reverberations throughout her entire body?

'Good news,' he said serenely. 'The Communists holding your husband and Miss Cheng were discovered this morning, purely by chance. There was a short fight and . . .'

Her heart stopped beating. 'Is Linc safe?'

'In fine fettle,' Mr Reidman crowed. 'Both he and Miss Cheng are unharmed. Do you have a television set?'

She gave the receiver a tiny shake of annoyance. What was the silly man talking about? What did television matter at this time? Linc was safe, she thought rapturously. Without warning her legs turned to jelly and she grabbed the nearest chair before they gave way. 'Yes, I have a television.'

'The English news will be coming on in five minutes' time. There'll be a short interview with your husband from the Bangkok studios. He's been trying to ring.' He sighed impatiently. 'And so have I. I've been trying to get in touch with you most of the afternoon. Didn't your maid pass on the message?'

'No, no, I've been out,' she stuttered. 'I've received no message.'

'Strange, your maid kept repeating that she understood, though to be frank I didn't grasp much more of what she said.' He gave an apologetic laugh. 'I'm sure your husband will be phoning again as soon as possible, though the lines from Thailand can be rather unreliable. He'll fill you in on the details. I'll ring off for now, Mrs Cassidy, and allow you to watch him on television.'

'Yes, thank you.'

In a daze Judith replaced the receiver. When she switched on the television set the screen lit up with the word *Berita*—news. Hunched up on the sofa, her eyes trained on the screen, she nervously twisted a strand of pale hair around and around her finger. Linc's free, she thought, her eyes wet with tears. He's coming back to me.

'And now we speak to the American pilot, Mr Lincoln Cassidy, who was taken hostage almost twelve months ago,' the announcer was saying.

Blinking rapidly, she stared at the screen. The camera had swivelled to a deeply tanned figure with shaggy dark hair, a beard and a moustache. She blinked again. 'Linc?' she whispered in bewilderment. The man was a stranger.

It *was* Linc. As soon as he smiled and started to speak she recognised him. The long hair and unruly beard had confused her, and he was wearing a disreputable-looking tee shirt and old jeans. He resembled some swarthy gipsy type, a romantic Che Guevara figure. Judith laughed. What a contrast! Before, Linc had always been impeccably dressed, the crease down his slacks razor-sharp, changing his shirt twice, sometimes three times, a day in the clammy heat. Regularly he had had his hair trimmed at the barbers' shop at the Sentosa Country Club. He had been clean-shaven, and once when he had experimented with a moustache, at her request, he had shaved it off after two weeks, complaining that it made him feel scruffy.

There was a slap of flip-flop sandals across the tiled floor. Over her shoulder Judith waved a silencing hand at Ah Fong, eyes and ears glued to the television.

'Missie, missie, Consul man phone,' the shuffling woman began, about to launch into a long-winded explanation.

'Sit down,' Judith hissed, patting the sofa. 'Look!'
She pointed at the screen.

Ah Fong's mouth dropped open. 'Mr Linc!' she said
reverently, then gave a great whoop of joy and clung to
Judith.

'Don't upset me any more,' she pleaded, half
laughing, half crying. Brushing a hand across her eyes,
she concentrated again on the screen. Linc was in the
middle of an explanation of how he and Kee-Ann had
survived over the past year.

'Would you care to give us your comments, Miss
Cheng?' the interviewer asked as the camera drew back
to reveal Kee-Ann sitting close beside Linc. Coyly she
cast down her almond eyes, then looked up and smiled.
Her blue-black hair was parted dead-centre, falling in
two glossy wings over high cheekbones. Fragile and
composed, she was so palely demure in contrast to
Linc's sunburnt virility.

'It was a great misfortune to be taken hostage,' she said
solemnly. 'But I was grateful Mr Cassidy was with me. He
was marvellous. He protected me, he kept me sane.' Her
voice had a slight American twang, the result of two years'
college in the States. Linc patted her hand benignly.

'Bad girl,' Ah Fong announced, sitting up straight.
'That one bad girl.'

'No, she's not,' Judith protested.

'Mimi say that one go in bars. Go with men.'

Judith sighed. 'She is nineteen, Ah Fong. It isn't a sin
to have a drink with a man at that age.'

'Bad girl,' the *amah* repeated flatly, tapping her ear.
'I hear stories. Bad girl.'

Refusing to embark on a futile discussion, Judith
devoted her attention to the screen. There was no doubt
Kee-Ann was a beauty. With her flawless complexion
and graceful gestures, she would bring out the
protective instinct in any man. The boys probably
flocked around her, and where was the harm? It was

only Ah Fong's strict Chinese upbringing which condemned the girl's more Western ways. Linc had warned Mr Cheng that his daughter's American education could alter her view of life, but it had not deterred him. She was following in the steps of three older brothers, all educated in the States, so her family knew what to expect.

'Some Western ideas, some Eastern, a good mix,' Mr Cheng had smiled.

When the interview was over Judith sat on the sofa, hugging her knees in delight. If only she and Ah Fong could speak to each other properly; she was bursting to discuss Linc's rescue with someone, but all she and the Chinese woman could do was repeat the same delirious phrases and hug each other. At length Ah Fong departed for bed, her beaming smile almost splitting her face in two.

Judith ran a flustered hand through her hair. Linc would be ringing soon, though doubtless it would take time for him to extricate himself from the television studios. Chewing at the fleshy inside of her lip, she wondered if there was time to telephone Wayne, then she laughed out loud, a laugh ringing with relief. Now there were no morbid decisions to make, nor that dreadful anniversary. Now she and Wayne could keep to their easy-going relationship, with no hidden strains. Now she was safe. The hand she stretched to the receiver stopped in mid-air. There was no point calling Wayne, he was in Sabah with Mr Cheng. It was tempting to phone Esther, but eventually she decided it would be inconsiderate; Esther always went to bed early when Wayne was away from home, in order to be fresh for Robbie if he awoke.

Hovering restlessly, she shifted from one foot to the other, feeling weak and shaky and lightheaded, and when the telephone rang she leapt forward, grabbing the receiver.

'Honey,' a loving, familiar voice said.

'Oh, Linc, I've missed you so much,' Judith gulped, and burst into tears.

'Hey, hey, Jude, be brave, honey.' His deep voice was soft like a caress, rolling over her and soothing her shattered nerves. 'I'll be home soon, though not for a day or two, and then we'll start all over again, I promise.' The line crackled, making her strain to hear his next words. 'I love you.'

'I love you, too.' She smiled through her tears, then she panicked. 'Why aren't you coming home straight away? Are you all right? Shall I fly to Bangkok?'

'Calm down, Jude. The Government officials here want to debrief me, that's all.' There was fond laughter behind his words. The line grew faint. Wrinkling her brow, she pushed aside the heavy ash-blonde hair and thrust the receiver even closer to her ear.

'It's just a matter of telling them all I know,' he continued. 'Don't worry, it's straightforward. There's no point your coming here because I understand I'll be held incommunicado. I'll ring you tomorrow evening— by then I should have a clearer idea of what's happening.' His voice faded.

'Linc!' she yelled.

'It's a lousy line, honey. Can you hear me?'

'Just,' she shouted.

She heard him laugh. 'It's great to speak to you again, Jude. How are you?'

'Fine, I've so much to tell you.' A sound like waves crashing on to rocks filled her ears.

'I'll ring you tomorrow,' Linc bellowed and the line went dead.

It was only when she felt the tears dripping off her chin that she realised she was still crying. Where was her stiff upper lip now? With shaking fingers she dialled the international operator and spent a frenzied, garbled half-hour passing on the news to her parents, who promised to fly out to visit her and Linc in a month or two.

She didn't sleep much that night. Hither and thither her mind rushed, planning the future, remembering the happiness she and Linc had shared. With lethal abruptness her stomach knotted. Oh Lord! she had forgotten to tell him about the baby. In all the excitement it had totally slipped her mind. Linc had been convinced she would conceive as soon as they decided to start a family.

'You're a fecund lady,' he had declared.

'How can you tell?' she had retorted, sticking out her lower lip in fake defiance.

He had made a grab for her. 'Something to do with the fact that you're very passionate. You'll get pregnant the first month. There'll be none of this sitting around for years like Wayne and Esther. I'm right,' he had insisted when she had looked doubtful. 'You'll see.'

He had been right. Her shaped brows drew together. Had the U.S. Consulate passed on the news of her miscarriage? She couldn't even recall if they had been aware of the reason for her spell in hospital; Wayne had dealt with them at that stage. Searching for a cool stretch of sheet, she rolled over to the edge of the bed. It was so hot. Despite the air-conditioner and the circling fan above her head, the atmosphere was stifling. She had stripped naked as usual, but her skin was still clammy. As she moved the mattress undulated beneath her. It was a water-bed. Linc didn't know about that either, she realised with an impish grin. It had been ordered before his trip into Thailand with Kee-Ann and delivered long after his disappearance. Eventually she fell asleep, but it seemed only minutes later that Ah Fong was banging on the bedroom door, shouting 'Telephone, missie, come quick!'

A glance at her wristwatch revealed it was scarcely dawn. Dragging on her blue silk kimono with its

embroidered dragon snarling on the back, she stumbled
out into the living-room.

'Ju*dith*!' a voice shrieked as she lifted the phone.
'Isn't this fabulous news! My boy's been freed.'

Last night she had taken the coward's way out and
decided she was too emotionally overwrought to cope
with Magda. Indeed, after speaking to her parents she
had gone straight to bed. Shaking back her hair, she
forced herself awake. Today she must get organised. It
was a blessing Linc had contacted his mother, she
would have been furious if the news had come from
another source.

'Lincoln sounds so healthy,' Magda crowed. 'I always
knew he would surge through victorious, it's his genes,
you know.'

'Oh yes?' She tried not to sound too disbelieving.

'Perhaps he'll be given a medal and we'll all have to
go to the White House,' Magda trilled, and Judith
could almost hear her choosing which outfit to wear to
wow the President.

'I doubt it.'

'He's promised he'll come over to California within a
week or two.'

'That's nice,' she agreed guardedly. Magda would
demand a tour of triumph; this blaze of glory would be
too good to miss. Doubtless even now she was planning
some celebration, a noisy dinner where she could hold
court. Perhaps Suzanne from Palm Beach would be
invited; that would be typical of Magda's unthinking
ways. Judith pulled a face at the telephone. Linc could
go alone, she decided with an unusual display of bad
temper. She was damned if she would desert the shop
only to waste time paying lip service to Magda's phoney
extremes of emotion. As quickly as the thought entered
her head, she rejected it. No way would she agree to
Linc flying off without her. From now on, if he went
anywhere they would go together. She accepted that a

trip to the States was inevitable. Magda *was* his mother, after all, and it was only right she should see him. She smoothed down the silk of her kimono as Magda gushed on, her voice rising and falling as she described how she had scarcely survived the impact of the news of her son's release.

'We'll come and see you soon,' Judith said, breaking into the flow. After we've had some time on our own, she vowed. Reluctantly she accepted she would be forced to desert Mandarin Antiques for a while. It would be regrettable with business so good, but the only alternative was for Magda to visit them in Penang, and if she came when would she leave? The Sentosa Country Club and its supply of male guests had proved a magnet in the past. Magda had sunbathed by the pool, still a fine figure of a woman at fifty-four, snaring any unfortunate gentleman who chanced to wish her good morning. And as her escorts had come and gone, so her visits had stretched like elastic. Linc had been forced to spell out loud and clear that she had outstayed her welcome and she had sulkily retreated, only to bounce back without recrimination, a month or two later.

'This catastrophe would never have occurred if Lincoln had stayed at home where he belongs,' she exclaimed indignantly. 'The Far East is much too dangerous, all those wild animals and creepy-crawlies.' There was a shuddering sound. 'I shall insist he returns to the States. You don't intend to make him move to England, do you?' she asked defensively.

Judith raised her eyes to the ceiling in despair. 'Linc's his own man, you should know that. I couldn't *make* him do anything even if I wanted to, which I don't. We shall plan the future together, and you can take it we'll be living in Penang for a good few years yet.' As far away from you as possible, she added silently.

Another year would see the shop firmly established.

Her mind flicked to the unit next door coming empty.
Why not spread her wings? She smiled at the idea. It
would be immensely satisfying to start a second
business from scratch.

Magda swept on as relentlessly as an avalanche. 'Hot
and cold goosebumps,' she was saying. 'I was so shook
up. When Cy came round he said he thought I'd seen a
Martian.'

'Who's Cy?'

'A very dear friend of mine. I was hysterical, I
collapsed into his arms and hugged him fit to bust.'

A brow arched. 'Poor Cy.' Magda didn't notice the
hint of sarcasm, she was too involved in her description
of how the neighbourhood had responded to the news
of her son's release.

'A reporter telephoned,' she continued gleefully. 'Cy
thinks they may ask me to be interviewed on television.
I wonder if satin looks shiny on the screen? Or perhaps
suede would be better? I have a dear little two-piece . . .'
Her voice faltered.

Judith smothered a giggle. Linc would go mad if
Magda appeared on television spouting her character-
istic blend of fact and fiction. It took several more
minutes for her mother-in-law to run out of steam.

'Linc will phone as soon as he arrives home,'
Judith promised, and gave a sigh of relief when the
line was cleared. Now that she was wide awake she
sat down and made a long list, then, bearing the time
difference in mind, started to telephone other relatives
and friends around the world, passing on the news of
Linc's release.

By the time she broke off halfway to eat breakfast,
her vocal cords seemed in danger of seizing up.
Swallowing a reviving mouthful of coffee, she glanced
at her watch. Rosiah would have to open Mandarin
Antiques on her own this morning, and no doubt she
would be wondering why her employer was late. This

was the first occasion since Judith had taken over the
shop that she had not been on hand to unlock the door.

'I have some more calls to make, Ah Fong,' she
explained, taking a bite of red watermelon. 'So when
you go to the shop, please tell Rosiah I shall be along
around noon.'

'I unnerstan',' Ah Fong grinned, delighted with her
young mistress's good fortune.

While the Chinese woman washed the breakfast pots,
Judith showered and dressed. She chose a loose voile
blouson in mulberry-bronze, teaming it with slinky
mulberry trousers. Fastening a chunky gold chain
around her neck, she sat down at the dressing-table.

'I go shop now,' Ah Fong called in through the open
bedroom door.

'Okay, see you later,' she replied, squinting into the
mirror. With a careful fingertip she applied a drift of
violet eye-shadow and added a line of kohl, making her
eyes seem enormous. She glanced down at her bare
arms. Once upon a time she had been a sun-worshipper,
gilded to a deep tan, but now she spent most of her time
indoors and the colour had faded to pale gold. She
grinned at her reflection. I'm radiant, she thought
joyfully. Her eyes were starry with happiness, her face
glowing. The tightness which had dragged at her
features over the past months had vanished overnight.

Returning to the telephone she checked her list. Local
calls next. 'Hello, Esther,' she said, introducing herself.

'Hi there, Judith. Hold on a minute, the baby's
crying.'

There was a clatter as the receiver was dropped and a
series of noises off. Half amused, half exasperated, she
tapped long fingernails on the polished table.

'Say hi to your Aunt Judith,' Esther instructed.

Silence.

Judith decided that if she waited for Robbie, at six
months, to say good morning, she would be waiting a

long time. 'I'm ringing to tell you Linc has been freed,' she explained, taking the initiative.

'How wonderful! I'm so happy for you. Wayne'll be real pleased.' For a while Esther enthused, making all the right noises, sharing in Judith's elation, then she stopped dead. 'Say, can you hang on another minute? Robbie's little eyelids are droopy. I guess he needs a nap, I'll pop him down in his crib. Back in a second.' There was another long pause. More noises off. When she returned to the phone Esther's tone was intimate. 'Do you think you could give me a clue as to what you and Linc did before you conceived so quickly?'

Judith laughed. 'I beg your pardon!'

'I don't mean to pry, but I wondered if you had some special theory. Wayne and I are eager for a second child and we'd like it to be real soon.' Wayne hadn't sounded eager at all, she remembered, but she remained silent as Esther chattered on. 'Have you any tips?'

'We did what comes naturally,' Judith assured her, grinning.

'You didn't check your temperature to see if the time was right?' Esther asked incredulously.

'No.'

'Now before I had Robbie . . .' She swept into a non-stop explanation of the whys and wherefores of conception. Shaking her head in disbelief, Judith listened patiently. First she had had to deal with Magda's effervescent ravings, now she was faced with Esther's obsession with babies. She wondered if she bored everyone silly when she started on her pet topic—Mandarin Antiques. Probably she did. 'I dare say you and Linc will have another child straight away,' Esther continued.

'No, not yet.' Rather to her surprise, she discovered her ideas had crystallised. 'I would like the shop to be solidly established before we have a family.'

There was a grunt from the other end of the telephone.

'I'm only twenty-seven,' she protested. 'I can afford to wait a year or two before I embark on motherhood.'

'But you and Linc wanted a baby.'

'Yes, we did *then*, but circumstances have changed. Now I'm involved with business matters.'

'Children are so fulfilling, much better than some mouldy old furniture.'

Judith resisted the urge to defend her precious antiques. 'I'm sure that's true,' she replied equably, 'but . . .'

'Must rush, Robbie's crying again,' Esther gasped.

With a wry smile Judith replaced the receiver. She was dialling the next number on her list when she realised she had forgotten to mention the weekend visit to the bungalow. Her brow furrowed. Events had superseded the arrangement; should she cancel the invitation? As the next number rang out she decided to stall. It was Friday. Linc had said he wouldn't be home for a couple of days, so it seemed likely it would be Monday before he reached Penang. Wayne and Esther's company would help make the weekend pass quicker and it would be fun to share her joy. She decided to let the arrangement stand.

It was early afternoon by the time she arrived at the shop. 'Sorry I'm late,' she croaked, rubbing her throat.

Rosiah smiled. 'No problems, everything has been running smoothly, and what wonderful news!'

Another dose of congratulations followed; they were becoming repetitive. It was something of a relief when she had finished her now well-worn recital of Linc's release and could concentrate on business. Mr Lim's promised delivery had been made, and after rapidly perusing the post, she devoted her time to the two large packing-cases. The pewterware was set aside, and then she separated the remaining knicknacks. Odd items were only fit for the 'bargain' tray, but she discovered several interesting copper gongs which would bring a fair price when Ah Fong had polished them, and there were also one or two pieces of intriguing old Chinese pottery.

Now the future stretched securely ahead and she hummed to herself, smugly fantasising over the happiness she and Linc would share, and the success of her business. Later in the afternoon she went next door to speak to the record shop owner. It transpired he intended to vacate the premises within the next fortnight, but had no knowledge of a successor. Judith decided that on Mr Cheng's return she would sound him out about acquiring the lease. She saw a gaping need for a high-class gift shop in the arcade. A friend had been pressing her to sell lengths of colourful hand-printed batik but so far she had had to refuse through lack of space. If she took over the unit next door her stock could widen dramatically. There were so many beautiful souvenirs tourists could glean from Penang—exotic pieces of coral, filigree silver, table mats woven from the leaves of the *mengkuang.*

When Rosiah left at six, Judith stayed on. She was determined to have everything shipshape, leaving no matters outstanding, for once Linc was home she would take time off, and she wanted to be able to do so with a peaceful mind. Idly she wondered how long it would be before he returned to flying. Perhaps after his twelve-month break he would want to ease back into it very slowly?

The tropical night air was warm on her arms as she parked the small car outside the bungalow. Pausing on the porch for a moment, she hugged herself in delight. How wonderful the world seemed now that Linc was coming home! Sweet fragrance from a nearby Cape Honeysuckle filled her nostrils and she took a heady breath. Her life was starting afresh. Languidly the breeze stirred among the paper-lantern blossoms of purple and white bougainvillea sprawling from huge earthenware pots on either side of the doorway. Judith inserted the key, and a spasm of doubt crossed her face as she discovered the lock had not been secured. She was sure she had turned it that morning, but warily accepted she *could* have forgotten. The high she was riding on meant anything was feasible. Normally she would have staked her life on her reliability, but she was forced to concede that in her state of dazed exhilaration she could have neglected to lock up.

Pushing open the door, she realised that two ceramic table lamps were lit in the living-room. Her brow wrinkled. Had Ah Fong called in? It seemed unlikely, and in any case she always came and went by the back entrance, which opened on to her room and the kitchen at the rear of the building. Judith paused, listening. All was quiet. Perhaps the *amah* had visited the bungalow earlier and had then been called away to deal with a family crisis. It had happened before. She frowned. It had been an exhausting day and no doubt the highly-charged condition of her emotions was making her read far more into the situation than it warranted.

She jettisoned her worry, making a point of locking the door behind her. Briefly she leant against it, soaking in the pleasure of the room. Since taking over Mandarin Antiques she had added a few more treasures to her home, and she had not finished yet. The furnishings were a confident mixture of old and new; the cool modern lines of a green-gold sofa and chairs complementing the rich carvings on rosewood chests and tables. Thick Chinese rugs were scattered in profusion on the white terrazzo floor. Snapping off the switches beneath the huge golden shades, she made her way through the darkness to her room.

As she undressed, she yawned. A cool shower would wash away the stickiness of the day and after Linc had phoned she would drop into bed. Tonight she knew she would sleep. She walked through into the en suite bathroom and as she stepped beneath the jet of water she thought she heard a sound. Lifting the edge of her shower cap, she freed an ear and listened intently, but there was only the soft thrum of the water. Her imagination was on overdrive, she decided with a self-deprecating twitch of her shoulders. She stepped back beneath the shower and started to soap herself.

Abruptly she stiffened—wasn't that another noise? Heart fluttering like a berserk butterfly, she switched off the water and waited. Nothing untoward, only the usual background noises of the tropical night—the spasmodic high-pitched clicking of geckos hidden in the eaves, the distant grumble of a bullfrog. It's those nerves of yours, girl, she admonished, you're wound up too tight. Cool water pounded down on her skin as she washed off the soap. She dried herself with a thick towel and shrugged into the forget-me-not blue kimono. With steady fingers she fastened the belt around the narrowness of her waist, then, sitting down on the dressing-stool, she began brushing back her hair. There was a bump in the living-room. Almost dropping the hairbrush, Judith stared in terror at the bedroom door. Someone was out there. Now it seemed a cast-iron certainty that the front door had been left unlocked all day. Anyone could have walked in. Her stomach somersaulted. . . .

She was alone. Doubtless Ah Fong was still at the *kampung*; she was not due for another half-hour at least. The bungalow had a large garden separating it from its neighbours, so any screams for help would go unnoticed. Her frightened eyes swept the room, searching for some means of defence. They settled on a highly polished iron, sometimes used to prop open the door. It was made of brass with a wooden handle—solidly heavy. Surely she could throw that at the unsuspecting intruder and make a dash for freedom? There was no sense sitting here trapped in the bedroom like some rabbit caught in the glare of headlights waiting to be mown down. Tiptoeing silently across the parquet floor in her bare feet, she hoisted the iron into her arms, taking a firm grip. She switched off the light, waiting for a moment as her eyes adjusted to the gloom. Now she and her enemy were equal, both in the dark.

There was another noise from the living-room. The intruder appeared to have charged into some piece of furniture and was muttering beneath his breath. Now was the time for attack. Flinging wide the door, Judith rushed out, brass iron raised on high. The room was inky-black, the windows shuttered. When she heard a soft intake of breath she steered unerringly towards it, heart thumping fortissimo. Silhouetted in the darkness was a tall figure.

'Get out of my house,' she yelled at the top of her voice, suddenly no longer afraid, now furiously angry. She hurled the iron forward.

'Jeez!' The figure staggered back beneath the impact. 'What the hell are you playing at, sugar?'

The voice was familiar. 'Wayne!' she breathed, relief sweeping over her like a flash flood. She switched on a table lamp, golden light filling the room.

Wayne was doubled over, clutching the iron at his stomach where it had hit him, gasping in shock. 'An inch or two lower and we could have been in dead trouble,' he grinned, glancing down.

Judith didn't like the way he used 'we', it didn't imply him and Esther. Her lips tightened. 'What are you doing here?' she demanded.

'I came a day early to keep you company.'

'I'm perfectly fine on my own,' she retorted in exasperation.

He shrugged her words away. 'While I was waiting I decided to take a shower,' he explained, as though it was the most natural thing in the world. He set down the iron. 'I thought I heard you arrive home, so as soon as I was dressed I came out, only to discover you'd doused the lights. I was hunting for the switch when I stubbed my toe in the dark.'

She eyed him suspiciously. 'You look very trendy. Is that a new shirt?'

He grinned at her. 'Do you like it?'

She had to admit the unfamiliar shirt was rather splendid. It was in midnight blue, with full sleeves and his initials monogrammed on the pocket. His slim black trousers looked new, too. His fair hair had been combed damply back from his wide brow and there was a cloying aroma of aftershave, too lavishly applied. Spreading his fingers at his hips, he rocked back, eyes narrowed as he assessed her. When she realised he was mentally stroking her beneath her kimono her temper began to bristle. A showdown was unnecessary now, with Linc due home, but if he pushed her too far . . . Impudently his eyes roved over her, and the silk robe suddenly seemed too revealing. With a determined hand she adjusted the collar, all too conscious of the naked curves of her body beneath the fine fabric. Wayne made no move. He was standing still, smiling at her. He was *too* still.

There was a sound from the kitchen, a key turning in the rear door. 'That'll be Ah Fong,' she declared, moving quickly away so that he wouldn't read the relief in her eyes. 'Would you like a drink and a bite to eat? I'll ask her to prepare something.'

'A drink sounds great, and perhaps a sandwich. I've flown here direct from Sabah, so I missed out on dinner.' He grimaced down at his sore toe. 'I'll go and find my shoes and socks while you're organising things.' He grinned at her and turned away into the spare bedroom.

Judith hesitated. She hadn't handled that very well.

The wisest strategy would have been to tell him to leave straight away, friend or no friend, but instead here she was, offering him her hospitality. Still, Linc would be home soon and Wayne would no longer be a danger. She tightened the sash at her waist. She would allow him a quick drink and send him on his way. Setting her mouth into a determined line, she strode towards the heavy swing door. The quicker her hospitality was despatched, the quicker Wayne would be gone.

Snapping on the kitchen light she gasped, her hand flying to her throat. Ah Fong was nowhere to be seen; instead a masculine figure was straightening up from the door at the far end of the room. Blood pounded, rushing to her throat, choking her. He was an alien figure, tall and muscular in a clinging navy tee shirt and faded denims. A tramp, her brain assessed blindly, frozen in horror. Everything was happening in slow motion, as he prowled towards her, soft-footed in worn sneakers. He stretched out his arms. For a stunned moment she gazed at him wide-eyed, then he smiled and a message staggered from her eyes to her brain-cells. 'Linc!' she breathed, hurling herself into his embrace.

'Jude, my Jude. My love, my darling, my rain, my sunshine, my life,' he murmured, stroking her hair as she clung to him laughing and crying, not knowing where she was or what she was doing. Only one thing mattered—Linc had come home. There was a lump in his throat, tears in his eyes, as she sobbed out her joy.

'I've missed you so much, it's been awful,' she wept.

'I know, my darling, I know,' he whispered, holding her tight, kissing away her tears with words of love and comfort.

'I thought you were a tramp,' she gasped, wiping the wetness from her face with her fingers. 'You're so . . . so hirsute.'

The lips against her brow moved into a smile. 'Is that one of your odd English words?' he teased.

'It means shaggy and untrimmed.' She touched the glossy whiskers on his jaw with a cautious hand.

'Don't you like my beard?' he asked, arching a thick brow.

'I don't know. You don't look like you any more.' She narrowed her eyes, inspecting him.

'It'll add a new dimension to our sex life,' he prophesied with a chuckle. 'Kee-Ann reckons it's groovy.'

She wiped away her tears, recovering by degrees. 'Is Kee-Ann home too? Why are you here, I thought you had to be debriefed? Why didn't you ring me? Was a special plane laid on? And how did you get into the bungalow, anyway?' She paused for breath as the questions rushed through her mind. There was so much to ask, so much to tell—they had twelve months to catch up on.

Linc started to laugh. Held in the circle of his arms, she could feel the seductive movement of his body, breathe the heady masculine smell of his skin. He's so big, she thought wonderingly, I'd forgotten how big he is, and how muscular. She twisted her arms tighter around his neck, melting against him, remembering the lovemaking they had shared.

'Cool it, cool it,' he grinned, the dents in his cheeks deepening beneath the unfamiliar coat of hair, the warm amusement in his eyes indicating he had sensed her sudden desire. He bent to kiss the sensitive hollow below her ear. 'I'll try and answer everything, honey, but give me a break. What with all the pressure from the media and the Government officials, then the flight and now your questions, I'm becoming dizzy.' He lowered his voice to whisper in her ear. 'And real horny.'

She laughed with delight, then pushed back from his arms. 'Are you hungry? Do you want something to eat?'

He had lost weight. There wasn't an ounce to spare

on his tall frame, just rippling muscles, teakstained by the sun. 'All I want is you,' he replied, pulling her firmly back against his chest. 'I want to hold you, feel you next to me. Now, just relax and listen.'

Judith swayed against him, resting her head against his shoulder, and as he began to talk she inspected him, feeding off the look of him. Her heart still caught at the full softness of his mouth, the brown yellow-flecked eyes with their fringe of thick dark lashes. Most of the time he did look like the old Linc, but suddenly his expression would alter and he took on the appearance of an interloper, some stranger masquerading as her husband. Her brows pulled together; it was the beard and moustache which were unsettling. Tomorrow she would ask him to shave them off.

'There wasn't much to give the C.I.A. boys or whoever the hell they were,' he was saying. 'The group which took us hostage were pretty inept, small fry politically. They weren't evil men, just incompetents.' He shrugged. 'After two hours this morning there were no more beans to spill and I thought "screw you, buster" I'm going home to my gorgeous wife. If they need any further information they can always fly over to Penang.'

'So you walked out?'

A crease appeared at the corner of his mouth. 'Let's say I persuaded them to see things my way.' He lifted his fingers to her jaw, following its smoothness as though relearning the contour. 'You're beautiful,' he murmured.

'And what happened next?' she insisted. She could feel the hardness of his chest against her breasts as sensitively as if they were both naked.

'Kee-Ann and I took the next scheduled flight from Bangkok. The U.S. Consul laid on a car at the airport here and they dropped me off before taking her on up to the Country Club.'

'How is she?'

His eyes hooded to produce the illusion of a stranger. 'Her usual East-West self,' he replied enigmatically. After a moment his face cleared. 'I called you when we landed to give warning of my arrival, but there was no reply.'

'I was at the shop.'

He kissed her temple. 'Audrey's working you late.'

Smiling to herself, she allowed the comment to ride by. When he had given her all his news, then she would reveal her role in Mandarin Antiques, and her success. 'How did you get into the bungalow?' she asked again.

'I remembered Ah Fong keeps a spare key beneath that pot of mother-in-law's tongue on the back step.'

'Magda phoned at the crack of dawn,' she said, grinning at the association of ideas.

Linc shook his head in mock despair. 'Don't tell me. I had enough of the dramatics when I spoke to her last night, but I believe I managed to stave her off. Let's skip that topic for now.' He nuzzled at the curls of ashen hair on her brow. 'I decided to creep in and surprise you, but you beat me to it.' His long tanned fingers trickled down her jaw to her throat, lazily stroking the warm skin, quickening the pace of her blood. Judith's heart began to spin giddily. Inching aside her robe, he brushed her collarbone with a feathery kiss, then burrowed his hand into the thickness of ash-blonde hair at the nape of her neck, coiling the long strands around his fingers, dragging her closer. 'Jude! I've missed you so much,' he said fiercely. 'I've nearly gone crazy wanting you. Now I need to get to know your body all over again.'

His abrupt intensity took her by surprise. Linc had never been intense. Ardent? yes, loving and eager to make love, but this thread of desperation, this raw yearning in his voice was new, she thought uneasily. In the past he had been relaxed, supremely confident of acquiring what he wanted and prepared to wait until it dropped into his lap, as it always did.

'Jude,' he muttered again. 'I want to make love to you, I *must* make love to you.' His mouth swooped down. For an instant Judith was taken aback as an alien moustache scraped across her skin and thick hair rubbed on her jaw. With scarcely contained violence he teased her lips open and as his own lips roamed her mouth, she quivered. Despite her bewilderment she felt herself gradually succumb to the passion which flowed through his touch. Even if this wasn't the man she remembered, he was still capable of arousing her to a heady pitch of emotion which made her body strain to his, made her breasts tingle with desire.

'Slip off your robe,' he murmured, his mouth leaving hers. His breath was hot on her neck. 'Let me look at you.'

'But we're in the kitchen,' she said, suddenly shy, suddenly afraid.

'I don't care.'

She could feel the leashed need within him as he tunnelled his hands through the hair at her temples and kissed her again, his mouth greedy. For an instant her desire flared with his, like a flame whipped by the wind, but when he released her and gazed steadily down into her eyes, it was as though she hardly knew him. He was a stranger, a demanding sensual stranger. Somehow their relationship had moved on to a different plane and the awakening realisation disturbed her.

'Take it off, please, honey.' His voice was slurred, his eyes heavy with desire.

Avoiding the fever of his gaze, she fumbled at the knotted sash. His command was mesmeric, she was in his power, but her fingers were lifeless, unable and half unwilling to untangle the knot.

'*Hell!*' he exploded. 'I'll do it.'

Judith trembled. She wasn't ready to be inspected by

this ... this hairy newcomer. Perhaps later her hesitancy would dissolve, but right now she needed a breathing space. Everything was happening too quickly. She frowned as he bent his head, the thick brown hair curling around his neck. If only she could calm him down and change him into Linc—easygoing Linc, her beloved husband. From out of nowhere came memories of the baby. 'I have something to tell you,' she said as his fingernails tore at the knot.

'Later, honey, later,' he insisted, the raggedness of his breathing seeming to fill the room as he tugged desperately at the sash.

She sensed that in a moment he would lose what precarious patience he possessed and rip the robe from her. 'It's important, you must know,' she insisted, pulling away from him. 'I'm very sorry, but ...'

The door from the living-room was thrust wide. Linc's head jerked up, his fingers stilled.

'What's taking so long, sugar?' Wayne was asking as he strode forward. 'A man can't wait for ever.'

CHAPTER THREE

LINC's expression hardened, his eyes razor-sharp as they swung from Wayne to Judith and back again.

For a split second Wayne was in shock; then, recovering quickly, he smiled. 'Linc, old pal, this is a surprise.'

Drawing back from her, Linc leant nonchalantly against the work surface and folded his arms, the gleaming muscles rolling to give a momentary illusion of molten bronze. The response was clipped. 'I bet.'

Wayne's smile crumpled and he cleared his throat. 'I hardly recognised you with all that hair. You're thinner, too.'

'And harder,' he was informed curtly.

A long empty moment followed. A moment in which, with sickening clarity, Judith could see the frozen cameo they presented—she and Wayne alone in the bungalow at night, she clad only in a thin robe, naked beneath it. Snatching at her scattered wits, she pivoted. 'Where's Esther?' she demanded. It was an effort to salvage some propriety, but she knew she was wasting her breath. From the moment she had come face to face with Wayne earlier she had unconsciously accepted that he had come alone. Anyone could tell he was not wearing the persona of husband and father this evening, for his stance was too much the rogue male, his svelte appearance too much the man on the make. She saw that the silky shirt had been unbuttoned to reveal a gold medallion swinging on his chest.

'Esther couldn't come.'

'Bad luck.' Linc's voice cut like a whip.

Judith babbled on, desperate to justify the situation.

57

'You were supposed to come and stay tomorrow, the three of you.' She turned to Linc. 'Wayne and Esther have a baby boy called Robbie. He's six months old.'

'Congratulations.' There was no offer of a hand, no friendly pat on the back, instead he kept quite still as he monitored Wayne from head to toe, the arrogant scrutiny forcing the object of his inspection to flush uneasily.

'This is some surprise. I had no idea you'd been freed,' Wayne mumbled, rubbing his hands together in a feeble attempt at jollity.

'That's obvious.'

Judith winced. If only Linc would stop the stabbing cryptic comments which said nothing and meant everything. His brown gaze swung to her and, to her fury, she felt her own colour begin to rise. There was no reason for her to have a guilty conscience, wasn't she the innocent party? Weren't both she and Wayne innocent? From somewhere deep within she summoned up the courage to silently contest the emotion simmering in her husband's heavy-lidded eyes. Should she blurt out that nothing had happened, nor ever would have happened, between her and Wayne? Or was she reading too much into his attitude? With nerves twanging taut like guitar strings, it was a struggle to decide whether or not her senses were playing her false. She frowned. Did he think she had been untrue to him?

Linc's eyes fell to her burgeoning breasts beneath the blue silk. 'I suggest you change into something decent and we'll all have a reunion drink,' he said, and smiled. 'I could murder a gin and tonic.'

Relief flooded through the room like a waft of fresh air. If they had been on the hook, he was graciously releasing them. For a moment he hesitated, then he made for a fridge at the far end of the room. Judith watched him go. Linc never walked, he prowled. He glided, like a wild cat, relaxed but alert, muscular arms held a little away from his body, making no sound in the soft-soled shoes.

'I'll rustle up something to eat, if you'll tell me what to do,' Wayne offered, his gratitude at Linc's change of mood undisguised.

Judith found pâté and crispbread, then fled into the bedroom. She pulled on briefs and a bra, covering them with blue jeans and a thick cotton-knit white top with a high slashed neckline. Now the contours of her body were carefully concealed. Slipping into white leather mules, she made her way back across the living-room. Fully clad, in high heels, she felt more than a match for whatever innuendoes Linc might decide to toss her way. She would make him understand, beyond all doubt, that Wayne had been a friend, a good friend, but that was as far as it went.

It was consoling to discover the two men talking together peaceably as she returned to the kitchen, and she decided she had misinterpreted Linc's critical air. After twelve months away from civilisation his social graces were bound to be a little rusty. He had been out of touch for so long, it would take time to ease back into the old camaraderie. He was slicing a lemon for their drinks, while Wayne energetically plastered the crispbread fingers.

'You've moved everything around,' Linc complained without looking up. 'Where the hell do you keep the tonic these days?'

With a plunging heart, she realised he was using the knife like a machete, chopping savagely at the lemon, and the idea struck her that he could be imagining it to be Wayne, or her . . .

'There's a second fridge now. You always used to say we needed more cool space,' she replied, keeping her tone carefully neutral though she was frowning at the resentment in his voice. Time had not stood still while he had been held hostage, surely he realised things would have changed? 'The drinks fridge is out in the passage at the back,' she continued brightly. 'Wayne got it for me secondhand.'

'Good for Wayne.'

She glared at her husband's broad back. They hadn't seen each other for twelve months, and now, when by rights they should be deliriously happy, he seemed to be spoiling for a fight. He hadn't been wrong when he had said he was harder, she thought angrily. Making her way out to the passage, she threw him a furtive glance. The fragmented lemon lay on the chopping-board, and when he reached across for a cloth to wipe his hands he stilled, sensing her inspection. Their eyes clashed. For a moment Judith was paralysed, then, lowering her lashes, she hurried on. Before, she had always had a fair idea what Linc was thinking, but now his gaze was enigmatic. She didn't have a clue how his mind worked any more, and a curious air of constraint and stiffness filled her. Oh Lord! she thought with a sense of foreboding, everything has altered between us, we're heading for trouble.

'Ah Fong will be here soon,' she remarked, returning with the bottles already slippery with condensation. There was silence. Wayne kept his head down, concentrating. 'She sleeps here most nights,' she added.

A masculine brow arched. 'Isn't Wayne's presence enough?'

Little by little he was forcing her to lose her patience. She clamped the opener over the metal cap of the tonic bottle and ripped upwards. There was a clatter as the top spiralled on to the tiles. She glowered at Linc, who was lounging against a cupboard. He looked so damned arrogant with that great dark beard—like some all-powerful judge about to reach for the black cap. But he had elected to play the jury too, *and* he had not granted any right of appeal.

'She didn't know I was coming,' Wayne intervened, gazing at the huge hill of crispbread, thick with pâté. She passed him a plate and he began filling it with the fingers.

'Your car wasn't in the drive,' she accused, remembering.

'It's probably hidden away in the garage where no-one can see it,' Linc drawled.

'It is in the garage,' his cousin confirmed awkwardly.

He shrugged his shoulders, the movement an eloquent confirmation of his thoughts.

'What was the food like in the jungle?' Judith asked, setting plates and napkins on a tray. How's that for an inane comment? she thought to herself. She had said it in the same manner she would have enquired about the standard of the lunchtime buffet at the Kuala Lumpur Hilton.

His mouth twitched. 'Rice, rice and more rice. Not a can of caviar or a bite of smoked salmon in sight.'

That sounded like the old Linc, softly mocking, but when she glanced across she saw the humour had not reached his eyes.

'Was it tough?' Wayne asked.

'It sure as hell wasn't summer camp!'

Footsteps sounded in the passageway. 'There's Ah Fong,' Judith announced, pricking up her ears.

The door swung open. 'Mr Linc!' The *amah* bounded heavily across the room as fast as her short legs would carry her and launched herself into his arms.

'Hi!' He lifted her off her feet and swung her round, all restraint vanishing. Linc was laughing, his head thrown back, his teeth dazzling white in the tanned teak of his face. 'You've gotten heavier,' he teased, setting her down.

Judith looked on, envying their natural rapport.

Ah Fong's plump face was flushed with pleasure. 'You skinny,' she responded, jabbing him in the stomach. He gave a fake moan and doubled over. The *amah* examined his beard and frowned. 'No like.'

'You'll get used to it.'

'I unnerstan'.'

Linc flashed Judith a smile of complicity at the glib comment. For a moment it seemed as if they were back together on the same wavelength and, reassured, she moved to his side. His arm encircled her, resting possessively at the curve of her waist.

Ah Fong embarked on a garbled explanation. She would go back to the *kampung* now and tell her neighbours that Mr Linc had come back from the guerillas. Then she would telephone Mimi. She would sleep the night in her own house, but missie was not to worry, Ah Fong would be at the shop early next morning. She wound on and on, eventually bustling away down the passage, eager to rush home and spread the news.

'What was that about the shop?' Linc frowned, as they went into the living-room.

'She works for me at Mandarin Antiques,' Judith replied, setting down the tray on the glass-topped coffee table.

'For you?' Something in his tone made her wary.

Wayne grabbed a finger of crispbread. 'That's right,' he chimed in, taking a bite. 'Your wife's fast becoming an authority in the antiques field. She's a very bright lady.' He swept her a proud look and Judith felt forced to respond with a tentative smile.

Linc's eyes were thoughtful, watching the interplay. Dropping down on to the sofa, he stretched out his long legs. 'Tell me more,' he commanded, directing his words at Judith, but before she could open her mouth Wayne leapt into the narrative.

'Audrey moved away and Judith bought over the lease. If you remember the store was functioning okay, nothing special, but since she took charge it's done real well.' He pushed the last inch of crispbread into his mouth. 'I only wish I had a wife who was so enterprising.'

'I bet you do.' Linc was back to the cryptic comments. In desperation Judith thrust the platter of food at him. 'Not for me.' He brushed it aside with a vague gesture and leaned forward to add a measure of tonic to his gin. 'Where did you get the money for the lease? Did Wayne supply that *too*?'

His eyes were trained on her, totally ignoring his cousin. Assuming a nonchalance she was far from feeling, Judith sat down in an armchair opposite, needing for some reason to keep a distance between them. Her thoughts lurched. In her fantasies over the past months Linc had been proud and delighted when she had revealed the news of Mandarin Antiques, so why was he acting like a disapproving interrogator now?

Wayne laughed gaily, wiping crumbs from his mouth. He appeared unaware of the undercurrent washing around the room like a malevolent tide. How could he be so insensitive? To her Linc was a wild animal slowly circling his prey, choosing the right moment to pounce.

Wayne rushed thoughtlessly in. 'She sold the Merc.'

'I was speaking to my wife,' Linc snapped, and forced a smile. It was as though he was unsheathing his claws, showing them to his victim and then curling them back beneath his fur.

Goodnaturedly Wayne shrugged. 'Sorry.' He perched on the arm of Judith's chair and reached for another crispbread. She wished he would move away, his presence so close beside her spoke volumes. She could tell that Linc didn't like it; she could see it in his face.

'You sold my car?' he asked in a low voice. His eyes had caught hers, the yellow flecks sparking dangerously.

'It was *our* car,' she protested, wishing she could run for cover.

He took a mouthful of gin and surprised her when he grinned, the slashes in his cheeks deepening beneath the beard. 'You never liked it, you were always driving into drains.'

She slammed her tumbler down on the glass-topped table, making Wayne start at the crash. Linc never moved a muscle. 'I wasn't *always* driving into drains!'

Leisurely he ran the palm of his hand across his jaw, paying no heed to her outburst. 'So I presume we own that box-on-wheels parked outside the front door?'

'The Mini? Yes. What's wrong with that?' she demanded, her anger billowing inside her.

'And how do you imagine I shall be able to fit in?' he enquired, running his eyes over the muscular legs stretched out before him.

In normal circumstances she would have been forced to admit there could be complications. Linc's legs went on forever, and he always needed an aisle seat if he was to sit in comfort at the theatre. 'You'll manage,' she crackled.

'Perhaps you didn't consider me when you bought it?' he suggested calmly.

'I did,' she lied, and heard her voice squeak.

He was correct. She had been so eager to raise money for the shop that the choice of another car had been unimportant. When Wayne had mentioned that one of the helicopter mechanics wanted to dispose of his secondhand Mini, she had jumped at the idea.

Wayne shifted on the arm beside her. 'It's cheap on gas,' he protested. Gradually he was awakening to the disquiet pricking the air. He rose, took two or three shambling paces across the room, then halted, frowning down into his glass. 'Judith has worked hard and long at the shop. You'll be full of admiration when you see the improvements.'

Linc took another swig of his drink. 'I'm sure I

shall,' he replied, wiping his mouth with the back of his hand.

She flashed him a searing glance. Surely he could manage some word of praise, show a slight degree of enthusiasm?

Wayne soldiered on with the desperation of one bent on squeezing blood from a stone. 'She's doing well financially.'

'Yes, I'll soon be able to buy you a replacement Mercedes,' she jibed witheringly.

Linc thrust an arm across the back of the sofa. 'Gee, thanks.'

In the following pause, Judith heard the shrill of cicadas outside in the trees.

'How is Esther coping?' Linc enquired, raising the tumbler to his lips. Now he was pleasant, sounding interested, and the unexpected switch of mood shook her.

Wayne smiled halfheartedly. 'Robbie's a great little guy, but Jeez! she sure makes one helluva fuss over him. Our lives revolve around him now.'

'You're jealous!' Linc grinned.

There was an answering grimace. 'She's obsessed with him. It's a relief to get away from the house in the morning. She spends her days worrying if he's too hot or too cold, too fat or too thin. Goodness knows what'll happen when he starts walking, I guess she'll follow him around from morning until night. She never lets up.'

'Sounds like my mother,' Linc commented.

'Well, let's hope Robbie has an independent streak like you,' Wayne grumbled sulkily. 'Otherwise he's destined to wind up a real pampered mummy's boy.'

Judith twisted to look across at him. 'Perhaps if you stayed home and took more of a part in his upbringing you'd lessen his dependence on Esther.'

'Sounds like a great idea,' Linc inserted drily. 'Staying at home.'

Another double meaning! Judith poked at the slice of lemon floating in her gin and tonic.

'I was real sorry when Judith miscarried,' Wayne announced, downing the dregs of his drink.

Her head shot up, her heart weeping with sudden despair. Why on earth had he broached that subject now? Her fingers tightened around her glass. She had intended to tell Linc about the baby when they were alone, for it was a private sorrow, not something to be aired casually over drinks. Her heart chilled—what a callous way for him to learn about the loss of his child!

'Wayne, don't,' she pleaded in a choked voice, turning away in a movement of futility. He was tearing her into shreds without knowing it.

Coolly Linc reached forward to set down his empty glass on the table. 'It's okay, honey, I know. The guy from the Consulate told me.' He rose to his feet, pushing his hands into the pockets of the old jeans. 'It's late. I guess it's high time you went home, Wayne.'

'N-now?' his cousin stuttered, taken aback. He glanced at his wristwatch.

'Won't Esther be expecting you?' Linc drawled.

It was a loaded question, and Judith's breath got trapped in her throat.

'She sleeps in Robbie's room most nights,' he mumbled. 'She'll not care whether I'm home or not.'

Judith stood up. To her surprise she realised she didn't want Wayne to leave. He was solidly familiar, an ally against Linc, who was proving to be an unknown quantity. 'Surely the pair of you will want to discuss business in the morning? The bed's already made up in the spare room. It seems pointless for Wayne to drive all that way south, only to return first thing tomorrow.' Try as she might, she could not bring herself to meet Linc's eyes. She sensed, rather than saw, his shrug.

'Whatever you want,' he said indifferently. He prowled over to her, arranging a long arm around her shoulders, his hand hovering in the air above one breast. Lightly his tanned fingers caressed the full upper swell beneath the cotton-knit. Hypnotised, Wayne was watching every movement. Linc was spelling it out, he was a male animal, claiming his mate. Caught in the middle, Judith inwardly cringed. The touch of his fingers was too intimate, too possessive; right now he was a stranger. In a day or two when the tensions between them had gone, then she would welcome his caresses. For there *were* tensions. The first bubble of rapture had burst, and now the expected ecstasy of resuming married life after a year apart began to seem unrealistic. . . .

She knew her feelings were ambiguous. She loved Linc, but he had changed. The man beside her was no easygoing lover, he was a man who had lived on a knife-edge, who had been down to rock bottom—a hard man, a man she didn't know any more. It was Wayne who was her friend, her stalwart companion through thick and thin, not this sensual man beside her who was using her for some basic ritual of his own.

'I'll wash up,' she gabbled, moving away.

Wayne rushed to her aid, loading the tray with dirty plates and glasses.

Linc's mouth twisted. He yawned, stretching up his arms, the fluid movement raising the tee shirt to reveal a smooth strip of teak-brown flesh above the slim-fitting jeans. 'Then I guess I'll take a shower,' he declared.

As she completed the mechanics of washing up, Judith heard Wayne talking, but her mind was a mass of too many contradictions for her to pay much attention. He was churning on and on about Esther, how she had changed since Robbie's birth, how now he was the odd one out. Ignoring him, her heart began to race. Within minutes she was destined to be alone with Linc, or rather with the man masquerading as Linc. Suddenly she was petrified.

'So you see, things'll have to change,' Wayne was saying as he followed her through to the living-room.

Murmuring something she hoped sounded like encouragement, she snapped off the lights. For a moment Wayne was silhouetted on the threshold of the spare room, his lanky frame so dear and familiar that she had the sudden urge to rush to him and beg for protection. 'Goodnight, see you in the morning,' she heard herself say in a cool voice.

Her heart fluttered with foolish relief when she realised that Linc was still under the shower. His discarded clothes lay on the floor, and automatically she picked them up and started to fold them. As the splash of water from the bathroom ceased, she froze. Time was running out! With rapid movements she jerked out of her jeans and into a white silk nightgown. It was virtually unworn, part of her trousseau, for before she had always slept in the nude with Linc, but now . . .

She eyed the reflection in the full-length mirror. Somehow the low-cut nightgown appeared brazen, clinging too tightly to the outline of her full breasts and hips. It was an invitation. She ran her fingers across her brow, wiping away a glistening film of perspiration, and realised, with a start, that the shutters had been thrown wide and the room was warm with the tropical night air. As though sleepwalking, she sat down at the dressing-table and began brushing through her hair with long smooth strokes. Confused, she was waiting for something to happen, but she didn't quite know what.

'That feels better,' Linc smiled, coming out of the bathroom.

Secretly she watched him through the mirror. He was half-naked, only a towel slung low around his hips. His chest was broader, more tightly muscled than she remembered, and his waist firmer. He had always kept himself in good physical shape, but now his body was that of a man who had toiled hard and long. He looked powerful, his skin burnt dark by the sun, the sprinkling of hair scarcely noticeable on his limbs. As he towelled himself dry, he glanced across at her through the mirror and grinned. In confusion, she dropped her eyes and concentrated on brushing her hair with unnecessary vigour. 'How did you get on with the Communist insurgents?' she asked woodenly.

By keeping him talking she was grabbing time to compose herself; then she realised she was behaving like some virginal spinster and had to bite down hard on her lip to suppress an hysterical urge to laugh out loud at her stupidity.

'Fine, they were nice enough guys. There were six who guarded us, and we got to know them pretty well.' His hand stopped its methodical rub across the breadth of his shoulders. 'Too well, in fact. The instigator of the kidnap was arrested in the early days and after that the group went to pieces. A young Thai, Sumphote, took control, but he didn't have the ruthless streak necessary for guerilla warfare.'

Aghast, Judith swung to face him. 'The ringleader was arrested!' she said in amazement. 'Then why didn't they discover earlier where you were being held?'

There was a grimace. 'You know the Thai police, honey. They obviously never connected him with our disappearance and he didn't offer any information. After he disappeared we were kept on ice. The group kept hoping he'd come back and tell them what to do with us!' He shrugged. 'It was hellish nerve-racking. Kee-Ann and I hung by a thread for weeks, wondering if we were likely to be freed at any minute. The men all had guns and they were very jumpy,' he continued, walking into the bathroom. 'I was afraid if the police stormed the camp we would get shot up in the crossfire. It was not a pleasant prospect.'

'That sounds a classic understatement!'

'It is.' Linc reappeared, his hair combed back behind his ears. With grave eyes, he studied her. 'You used to be my golden girl, but now your skin is like champagne,' he said, rubbing one finger along the line of her shoulder.

'I spend a lot of time at the shop.'

His lips tightened. 'So Wayne said.'

'It's too warm,' Judith complained, hastily changing the subject. 'Why did you open the shutters? I sleep with the air-conditioner switched on.'

'I've gotten used to the natural climate. I don't think I can sleep if it's cool.' He raked the thick hair from his brow, and she noticed that it was almost dry, streaked by the sun. 'Mind you, I feel so damn weary I could fall asleep on the rim of a dime.'

'Why don't you lie down?' she suggested.

Beneath the tan his face was drawn, with dark shadows around his eyes. 'I want to lie with you,' he replied, reaching out for her and drawing her close. Even his touch was different, she thought with a flurry of apprehension, for as he bent his head to kiss her she felt his fingers biting into her flesh; they were hard and calloused, the touch of a stranger.

Standing stiffly, she tossed back her hair. 'Did you sleep in the open?' She knew she sounded like someone making conversation at a cocktail party, but she needed to talk and keep on talking.

'No, it was all fairly civilised. Kee-Ann had a hut to herself and I shared with the guys.'

The information had been impatiently given, and she was aware he was steering her towards the bed, his mouth warm and eager as he kissed the straight line of her shoulders.

'What was Sumphote like?' she asked brightly.

'Damn! *Jude*!' He released her and dropped down onto the edge of the bed, pushing his hands fractiously through his hair. The brown eyes were raised to hers. 'He was a bright guy, a university drop-out, full of high-flown political views.'

'And . . . and the others?' she stuttered.

'The rest of them were peasants, thick as two short planks and all the more dangerous for it.' Linc stretched his arms out behind him, leaning back, and as the bed moved he frowned. 'What's happened to this mattress?'

'It's a water-bed, don't you remember? We ordered it before . . . before you went away.' She gave a tentative smile. 'It takes some getting used to, but I think you'll like it in time.'

Linc pushed a large fist into the softness. 'I'm not sleeping on that! We'll sleep on the floor.'

'The floor!'

'Why not? I've been sleeping on a mat on the ground for the past twelve months.'

'Well, I haven't!' she flared, 'and I don't intend to start now.' Her blue eyes glittered. 'I shall sleep on the bed.'

'Like hell! You'll sleep with me *on the floor*.'

The situation was becoming grotesque, they were bickering like two fishwives. The humour suddenly seemed to strike Linc and he grinned. 'Honey,' he said, holding out a hand. 'The floor's not that bad. We can sleep on the sheepskin rug. We've made love on it before, if you remember.'

She ignored the outstretched arm. 'That's different.'

'I don't see how.'

Wearily she lifted the heavy weight of hair from her neck where her skin was moist with sweat. It was too late to quibble, and besides, she didn't think she could muster up a reasonable argument about such an emotional topic.

He smiled when she made no answer. 'I knew you'd see it my way.' He wore his male arrogance like a suit of shining armour, and she felt like weeping as he rose to his feet to claim her again. Linc always won in their battles. Before she had never minded too much, but now . . . Her mind seethed. If only he was flexible, like Wayne. Wayne always deferred to her wishes.

Linc was nuzzling her neck, whispering her name over and over again. 'Jude, Jude, my Jude.'

But I'm not yours, she wanted to yell.

'Relax,' he murmured, kissing the lobe of her ear.

'I *am* relaxed.'

'You're not, but you will be,' he assured her. He kissed her, nibbling seductively at her lips until her mouth opened of its own accord, allowing him access to gulp in her sweetness like a man finding an oasis after months in the desert. His intensity captured her again. Little by little, he was relearning her and she felt her body responding to his will. But he was 'someone else', she justified, trying to deny the blossom of desire budding within. Why did her flesh react so positively to this man's need? she wondered, half despising herself. Why? Her breathing quickened, her temperature began to rise. 'Linc,' she admonished, pushing herself a little away. 'It's well after midnight, shouldn't you get some sleep?'

He smiled down at her, watching the rise and fall of her breasts straining beneath the fine silk. 'I can sleep later, right now I want to eat you,' he declared with all the candour of a cannibal. He pulled her back against his chest and she felt the graze of his beard as his mouth resumed its erotic safari. Her blood raced. His kisses were sweeping her away and now there was no holding back. She knew that whoever he was, whoever he had become, she needed him. But how could she feel like this when half her mind was shrieking that he was a stranger? With masterly skill he was arousing her, kissing all the secret places which pleasured her so. Her brain stopped its protestations as she clung to him, giddy with desire. He lowered her on to the sheepskin rug, dragging the nightgown over her head. Now there was no restraint. Wantonly she thrust herself against him, her skin throbbing with the sensuous wanderings of his hands and his lips. Perhaps he was using her, but she didn't care. It was a two-way thing. After a year of enforced celibacy, her body was reawakening from its long sleep. Her skin was fevered, the sweat intermingling with his. Crimson stars exploded behind her eyes as this hairy Adonis lowered himself upon her, and her fingernails clutched at the iron-hard muscles of his back. Ruthlessly he was forcing her into a sensational whirlwind. She whimpered his name.

Linc's muscles tightened. 'Jude!' he said fiercely.

And then it was over.

She awoke to the weight of a long arm across her, pinning her to the bed. Its owner was fast asleep, lying on his stomach, his face buried in her hair. Instantly she came alive, keeping stock still, listening to the steady rhythm of his breathing. How did they come to be here? The last thing she could remember was lying with Linc on the sheepskin rug, drugged by their lovemaking. Carefully she reached for her watch on the bedside table. It was after nine, and a glance at the window revealed that the sky was blue and another sunny morning was well into action. There was the distant swish of the gardener's broom as he swept up the blossoms, the occasional zoom of a car on the road. Sweat was trickling down the back of her neck and between her breasts. Stealthily she edged her way out of his grip and Linc murmured, flinging his arms wide above his head. He slept on.

Judith tiptoed into the bathroom and closed the door. As she showered she remembered that the cases of Korean brassware were due that morning. There was no point staying at the bungalow, waiting around for

Linc to awaken; he might sleep all day. She could use the time far more profitably by going to the shop, just for an hour or two, to supervise the unpacking. Quietly she pulled on her clothes, wearing a floppy-sleeved blouse in sunshine yellow silk and jeans, topped by a studded denim waistcoat. Her make-up was quickly accomplished—pearly aquamarine eye-shadow, a brush of mascara and the briefest touch of rose-beige lipstick. She caught her hair to one side of her head, tying it around with a yellow chiffon scarf, the ends trailing over her shoulder. Fastening the straps of her high-heeled sandals around her ankles, she collected her bag from the dressing-table and tiptoed from the room.

'Hi.' Wayne, seated at the table in the dining-area, raised a hand in salute. He gestured towards the percolator. 'Want some coffee? It's freshly perked. I made some toast too.'

Smiling gratefully, she sank down. 'Thanks, but I don't feel hungry right now. I'll just take coffee.'

She cast a glance at the watermelon on Wayne's plate; even a mouthful of the cool porous flesh would choke her. She felt like a pricked balloon. In her daydreaming she had imagined Linc's return as days of love and laughter, sharing secret jokes, holding hands, being together. But they weren't together, not spirit-ually, for the past year had wrought changes and they were two different people. Their physical reunion had been a need dictated by the flesh, that was all. . . .

Wayne nodded in the direction of the bedroom. 'How is he?'

'Still asleep.'

He inspected his watch. 'It's possible he could sleep all morning. I dare say he's exhausted. I won't hang around right now, I'll go on home. Esther will be wondering where I've gotten to. When Linc wakes tell him to give me a buzz if he wants to talk helicopters.'

Judith watched him over the rim of her cup. He was tapping a nervous arpeggio on the tablecloth.

'What happened about the planes in Sabah?' she asked.

'I didn't commit myself,' he said. Then his face brightened. 'I'll have a word with Linc and see what he reckons we should do.'

'But he's out of touch. You can't expect him to take a decision like that with no knowledge of the background.'

'Oh, he'll be prepared to take control,' Wayne replied happily.

Linc had always taken charge, she mused, swallowing a mouthful of hot coffee. In retrospect she could see that their rare quarrels had inevitably been caused when her independent streak had clashed with his scheme of things. Linc's presence in her life had been as comforting as a thumb and a blanket, but occasionally she had been irked by his belief that, when it came to the crunch, he was the boss. In business Wayne was termed his partner, but in reality it was always Linc who made the important decisions, blazed the trail. Now Judith suspected unhappily that it had been the same in their marriage. She wasn't a partner either, she was one of his belongings, though a cherished belonging at that. He regarded her as 'the little woman', always doing silly things like driving into drains. She tightened her grip on the cup. Until today she had viewed their marriage through rose-coloured spectacles, but suddenly the past took on a different hue. . . .

When Wayne had gone, she cleared away the breakfast crockery and then poked her head around the bedroom door. The tanned stranger was spreadeagled on his stomach, a white sheet, even whiter in contrast to his darkness, tangled across his hips. He didn't belong in her bed, she thought with a look of resentment which noted the long hair, the beard on his jaw. Abruptly her stomach plunged and her fingers clutched at the edge of the door in panic. After last night there was a possibility she could be pregnant. Oh Lord, no! please don't let that happen, not yet. Last night she had been too emotional, too in need of physical satisfaction to spare a thought for the consequences, but now, in the glaring light of day, she realised the risk she had taken. On the last occasion she had conceived straight away. Judith closed her eyes in despair. She didn't want a baby yet, not while her life was still in the melting-pot.

The Mini started at the first turn of the key. It was always reliable, she thought defiantly, swinging out on to the narrow road. However scathing Linc might have been, it had proved to be a wise investment, and she had Wayne to thank. Tall casuarina trees waved their lace-fronded boughs as she drove by, and there was the occasional flicker of a sun-sparkled sea through the palms, a glimpse of vivid blossoms, of wooden *kampung* houses with their patterned-tiled steps and bright paintwork. The windows of the little car were wound right down, and the gentle breeze smoothed her brow, calming her. The pulses which have been jumping steadied and she began to relax. Linc's arrival had been more traumatic then she had supposed; it would take a little time to adjust. She slowed as an oxen-pulled cart turned on to the road ahead of her. There was no rush. They had all the time in the world to get to know each other again, and what better place to restart their marriage than in Penang?

CHAPTER FOUR

THE Korean brassware exceeded her expectations; it was a random mixture bought on spec, but her instinct that it would be a worthwhile investment had proved correct. There were beautifully worked lamps, bowls of all shapes and sizes, and a mass of tiny animals— dachshunds which doubled as bottle-openers, solemn owls, toads which looked so realistic that she was afraid they might leap to the floor. Ah Fong polished a selection when she arrived, and while Rosiah dealt with customers Judith did her sums, working out a selling price with a reasonable margin of profit. She arranged a gleaming display of the smaller items on the glass shelves, and within minutes an Australian couple had bought two of the dogs and were promising to come back later with friends. Judith thought again of the shop to be vacated next door; with extra space she could have a much wider selection of brassware.

'It's almost one o'clock. Is it okay if I go out for my lunch?' Rosiah queried, closing the cash register.

'Heavens, is that the time?' In dismay Judith gazed at her watch, hardly believing the position of the fingers. She had intended to ask her assistant to take an early break in order that she could rush home to Linc, but the morning had disappeared without her noticing it. 'Do you think you could be quick?' she asked. 'My husband has come home, and I'd like to get back to him.'

Guiltily she realised it was the first time she had mentioned him, her absorption in the brass had been so complete. Rosiah offered joyous congratulations and hurried away, out to the hawker stalls along the road which sold *nasi lemak* and *mee hoon*, the food there being a fraction of the price charged for meals in the hotel. The arcade was quiet; most of the hotel guests were at lunch, and Judith took advantage of the lull to go into the small store-room at the rear to collect an armful of the polished animals.

'J. Cassidy, proprietor, I presume?' a deep voice enquired, and she started in surprise, nearly dropping the lot. Linc was standing in the centre of the shop, feet planted firmly apart, hands on his hips as he casually surveyed the stock. She had failed to hear his approach in his soft sneakers. A couple of the ornaments clattered on to the marble floor.

'I . . . I didn't expect you,' she stuttered, thrusting the survivors on to a chair.

'Obviously not, but I *did* expect you to be at home.'

Avoiding his eyes, Judith bent down, and when she saw that one of the brass pieces had rolled beneath a desk she sank to her knees. 'You were asleep,' she said defiantly, risking a glance at him over her shoulder. 'I left a note on the table.'

'I didn't see it, but in any case I don't much care for waking up alone after all this time.'

Perhaps she had been wrong to desert him on his first day back, she realised uncomfortably, but there was no need for him to be so censorious. The feeling of guilt prodded her temper. 'You mean you prefer to indulge in semi-rape first thing in the morning,' she said icily, hearing the unkind intonation in her voice and hating herself for it. The brass animal had come to rest beyond her reach, and she was forced to stretch out an arm beneath the desk, head on one side, her hair brushing the floor. When her fingertips touched something solid, she edged forward.

'It isn't classed as rape if you have a willing accomplice, and you were always willing,' he retorted. 'But I'm grateful that you remember my habits. In future I expect you to be in bed with me when I awake.'

Her fingers clutched at the ornament, retrieving it, and she struggled to her knees. Line was towering above, one brow arched as he inspected her.

'You forget I have a shop to run,' she defended, scrambling to her feet.

His hand shot out to grip her chin. 'Let's get it straight, lady, from now on *I* come first. You've had your fun for twelve months, but now it's over.'

'Fun!' she gasped, her eyes round. 'Is that what you think it was?'

'I've no idea, I wasn't here, but if you imagine I'm prepared to take second place, like your friend Wayne,' he sneered, 'then you're sadly mistaken.'

'Wayne's your friend, too.'

His fingers were hard on her jaw, holding her firm. 'He *was* my friend. Whether he still is remains to be seen. He's a great guy, but I'm well aware of his peccadilloes.'

Her eyes were a stormy blue. 'Meaning?'

'Meaning Wayne has a vast capacity for seeing himself as a knight riding out to rescue a damsel in distress. And he's a sucker for long blonde hair and ...' His eyes dropped. 'And well-stacked dames.'

Judith's patience snapped. 'Oh, don't be so ... so American!' she said waspishly.

He gave a hollow laugh. 'Potato, pota*h*to, tomato, toma*h*to,' he recited. 'We went through that stage long ago. You knew what you were taking on when you married me, lady, so don't yell treason now.'

'You've changed,' she hurled.

'And so have you.'

His steady stare was beginning to unnerve her, and she lowered her lashes. It was the sound of conversation outside in the arcade that gave her the impetus needed to pull herself from his grasp. The Australians had returned, bringing with them another middle-aged couple. They were a well-dressed quartet, sporting fashionable outfits obviously purchased from some expensive store; the women in pastel-shaded sundresses with matching jackets, while their menfolk were crisp in poplin shirts and tailored shorts.

'Excuse us,' one of the women said gaily. 'We'd like to take another look at those gorgeous little animals.'

As her eyes fell on Linc, her expression altered into disapproval, and it was plain to see she was wondering how such an unkempt character had ever gained access to the luxurious interior of the Sentosa Country Club. Judith followed her look of outrage, and suddenly saw him through the same eyes. He was wearing the tight tee shirt and faded jeans he had worn the previous evening, and the breeze had blown his hair into disarray, curling it across his brow. As he rested his hips on the corner of the desk and idly crossed his legs, she noticed that the worn shoes were thick with dust. 'Did you walk?' she hissed as the customers turned towards the shelves.

'How else would I get here? I couldn't take a taxi—I don't have any money.'

The Australian woman cocked an ear as she toyed with the brassware.

'None!' Judith was surprised. He always carried a wad of notes in his wallet.

'Where the hell do you imagine I would get some?'

'I . . . I don't know,' she said lamely. It dawned on her that all he had was what he stood up in. She moved towards the cash register. 'I'll give you some; how much do you want?'

By now the woman customer was eavesdropping shamelessly, and Linc flashed her a sly look. 'Don't you think I should earn it, honey?' he purred. 'I don't like to feel you're keeping me.'

'I don't know what you mean,' she retorted, then noticed the humour curving his mouth and the fact that the woman was watching goggle-eyed.

'I'd hate folks around here to get the impression I was your. . . .' He paused significantly. 'Your gigolo,' he added, straightfaced.

There was a silent gasp in the background, and Judith scowled furiously, sending him all kinds of messages, but he ignored them as he smiled back with blithe indifference. She balled her fists. Already she could hear the scandal flying around the hotel restaurant—'That young woman in the antique shop has a . . .' The voice would hush, ears would strain. 'A lover, a rather wild individual, though goodlooking if you care for long hair and a beard. He must be a hippie, he's probably on drugs, that type often are.'

'Why don't you go to the barber's?' she demanded, grabbing a pile of *ringgits* from the drawer and thrusting them into his hand.

Linc made a great play of sorting the notes, then he carefully folded them and tucked them into the tight back pocket of his jeans. 'I'll need some new clothes, too,' he observed, watching the woman's reaction from beneath the thick fringe of his lashes. 'I tried on those in your wardrobe, but they don't fit too well. I'm broader across the shoulders than the guy who wore them last.'

'Lincoln!' she warned in a low voice.

Innocent as a cherub, he grinned when the Australians came forward with their selection of purchases. One of the men returned his smile, but the two women were stony-eyed, bosoms heaving in moral indignation. Judith wrapped the animals in tissue paper and popped them into small bags bearing the name Mandarin Antiques.

'It was real good of you to take me in last night

without warning. Not many women would have done that,' he murmured as she handed over the change. 'We sure made the waves break in that water-bed of yours!'

The quartet scuttled off, pausing to huddle together for a hasty exchange of views when they reached the far end of the arcade.

'You don't give a damn, do you?' Judith demanded, unable to curb her temper any longer. 'You think it's amusing to talk like that in front of my customers? Well, let me tell you it's taken sweat, toil and tears to make this shop successful, and I won't allow you to ruin its good name.'

'And what about tears for me?' he demanded, his humour running from him like water down a drain. 'You appear to have been so engrossed with this collection of—of . . .' he waved a casual hand, 'this collection of junk, that you haven't missed me.'

'That's not true,' she flared, her eyes suspiciously bright. 'I *did* miss you. I'd rather have you by my side than own a hundred antique shops.'

The dark eyes scoured her face. 'Prove it. Close up now and come home with me,' he ordered abruptly. 'From all accounts you've worked plenty of overtime in the past, you're allowed some freedom. In any case, it's Saturday.'

'Give me ten minutes and then I'll come,' she promised. 'Rosiah is due back soon, so let's wait until she arrives. There's no point closing for no reason at all.'

'No reason! *I'm* the reason.' She heard his voice harden. 'Come with me now.'

'But we're busy on Saturdays, Linc. I've been at the shop every weekend for months.' Her mind flew back to his work habits. 'You flew on Saturdays and Sundays when you were setting up your company.'

'I was single then. In any case, you can't compare

running a million-dollar aircraft business with looking after a single shop.' The jeering look faded, to be replaced by a coaxing smile. 'Jude, honey, we've been apart for twelve months.'

'Wait a few minutes,' she pleaded, 'then. . . .'

'No,' he snapped and strode off down the arcade before she had time to change her mind.

With a sinking heart she watched him go. In the past their quarrels had been heated clashes, dying as rapidly as they had flared, but now. . . . He had never walked out on her before, but then before she had never refused to meet an ultimatum. She sank down at the desk, her head in her hands. She knew she had been wrong in leaving him alone this morning, so why hadn't she gone home with him? What perverse streak had insisted she put Mandarin Antiques first when she knew, deep down, Linc was her one and only priority? With clenched teeth, she decided it had been his domineering manner which had made her stubborn. If he had asked her politely, as Wayne would have done, she would have hung up the 'Closed' sign in a flash. Or would she? The business had been her sole, all-consuming interest for so long, to neglect it would be like neglecting her own child. Couldn't Linc understand that?

By the time Rosiah arrived, ten minutes later, Judith had decided on the action she must adopt. 'I'm going home now and I won't be in tomorrow,' she announced. 'We'll advertise for another assistant next week, because I won't be spending as much time in the shop in future. If I'm not here any morning when you arrive, just go ahead and open up without me.'

There! she had said it, she thought rebelliously as she stomped away down the arcade. The first move had been made to detach herself from Mandarin Antiques, but it had been as painful as pulling skin from dry ice. She was marching down the shallow carpeted staircase into the entrance lobby when she caught sight of Linc. Her spirits soared—reprieve! He was deep in conversation with a young Malay.

She hurried to his side. 'Hello!'

'Hi.' Calmly he introduced her to the young man, who, it transpired, was a reporter from a local newspaper who was interested in Linc's experiences as a hostage and wanted to arrange an interview. 'How about tomorrow morning?' Linc suggested, throwing Judith a challenging look. 'My wife will be involved with her business, so I'll be free.'

'No, no. I'm not working,' she said hurriedly.

He took the news without comment, altering the interview to the following day.

'Have you been talking to him for long?' she asked, as the young man departed.

He took her elbow, steering her through the clusters of holiday-makers and out into the open air. Dazzled by the glare of the sun, Judith slipped on her dark glasses.

'I'd just met him. When I left you I went up to the penthouse to see Kee-Ann. She needs some support, she's been through a bad time. Don't forget we've shared the past year, we've become close.'

'And is she fully recovered from her ordeal?' Try as she might Judith found it impossible to keep the crust of chagrin from her voice. A small shiver touched her. It was clear that when she had refused to comply with her husband's wishes, he had gone straight to another woman. She tossed the chiffon scarf from her shoulder. What on earth was she thinking about? Kee-Ann was a child. The idea of Linc falling for a young girl was ridiculous. He was a mature man of the world; baby-snatching was not his scene.

The Mini was parked on the semi-circular drive which swept across the front of the hotel complex.

'Why don't we hire a boat and sail to Monkey Bay?'

he suggested as they approached. 'It's a great day, perfect for lying in the shade of the palms.'

Behind her sunglasses she kept as silent as death, working through the implications. She knew fine what Linc had in mind—more lovemaking. She had taken chances once, only a fool would do so again. 'But . . . but we don't have any swimming costumes with us,' she said weakly.

'Jude, you've become straightlaced since I've been gone,' he teased, smiling at her across the top of the car. 'But perhaps you're right. It's more fun if we go prepared with a bottle of wine and a picnic. We'll leave it for another day.'

Contrarily, his casual agreement to her unspoken wish now filled her with annoyance.

'Keys, please,' he demanded, stretching out a large hand. 'I'll drive.'

Obediently she sat beside him, cringing as he smashed his way through the gears and powered out on to the open road.

'It's like driving a pedal car,' he muttered. He had pushed the driver's seat back as far as it would go, but still his legs seemed too long. She had never considered the car to be small before, but now it seemed tiny, his broad shoulders filling most of the space, rubbing against her as he drove.

'When do you intend to buy some new clothes?' she asked, her eyes fixing on the frayed trouser leg of his jeans.

He shrugged. 'No rush.'

'And what about having your hair cut and removing that beard?'

A muscle clenched in his jaw. 'Stop bugging me, lady. If I shave off my beard in one fell swoop I'm going to be left with a two-tone jaw. It'll have to go in easy stages, when *I'm* ready, so be patient.'

Judith chewed at her lip like a reprimanded schoolgirl

as memories of the old Linc, the *true* Linc, re-reeled themselves in her mind's eye—Linc immaculate in his pilot's uniform, sleek in the dark suit he had worn at their wedding, athletic in his ski clothes, brimming with energy in tennis whites. She tossed a withering look at the casual interloper driving the car—*her* car.

'I was real cut up when I heard you'd lost our baby,' he said quietly, and she was filled with remorse at her unkind thoughts.

She stared at the hands clasped in her lap. 'It's over now,' she heard a distant voice remark. 'It all seems to have happened a long time ago, almost to someone else.' Tears were blurring her vision.

'Perhaps our lovemaking last night will show some results,' he murmured, glancing anxiously across at the tight profile.

'We didn't make love last night, that was lust,' she retorted with a defiant lift of her chin.

Linc sighed. 'It seemed like love to me, but what do you expect after twelve months—soft lights, sweet music and a long leisurely build-up to the action? Even Wayne couldn't manage that, which reminds me, where did he disappear to this morning? He promised to stay and bring me up to date on the choppers and the planes.'

'I don't think he actually promised.'

'No! now that I think about it, he didn't,' Linc drawled. '*You* were the one who was desperate for him to stay the night.'

Judith glared at him. For an instant he switched his attention from the road and what she saw in his dark eyes made her want to slap him. 'Wayne's been very kind,' she protested. 'You should be grateful.'

'Grateful! Grateful for what? Grateful he's been easing himself into my shoes while I've been gone?

Grateful he's neglected his wife and child in order to court you?'

'He's given me moral support, that's all.'

'Moral! That's a laugh,' Linc cut in, without a scrap of humour. 'He might act the innocent, flashing that toothy grin of his, but he doesn't have a moral bone in his body.'

'Don't be so critical. He's your cousin.'

'Sure he's my cousin, I can't avoid that, and I admit he's been a lifelong friend. He's a fine pilot, good company, and we've been through a lot of adventures together, but that doesn't mean I trust him. He was married too young. He forgot to sow his wild oats and now he's making up for lost time.'

'Not with me!'

He tossed her a glance. 'He's always maintained that if he'd seen you first he would have grabbed you.'

'You know that's a joke, Linc, he's married.'

'A fact which never worried him before,' he replied harshly.

'Oh! but you're cynical. You never used to be like this.'

'I'm realistic,' he remarked, swinging on to the red-chip drive of the bungalow. He parked beneath the covered porch and climbed out, stretching his legs with painful exaggeration. 'It'll have to go,' he pronounced, slapping the bonnet of the little car as he walked round to join her. 'I'll wind up arthritic if I'm forced to drive with my knees continually up to my chin.'

Judith managed to contain a sharp rebuke—just. He had verbally assassinated Wayne and was now disposing of the car. What was next in line for his firing squad—her?

'I'll make some lunch. How does prawn salad sound?' she asked in a bland voice.

'It sounds great.'

'I'll change into something looser before I start the preparations,' she said, making for the bedroom. 'This outfit is fine in the air-con, but it's too much in the heat.' Unlike the Sentosa Country Club, only the bedrooms at the bungalow had air-conditioners and these were too expensive to be kept running continually.

'Would you like me to slip into something more comfortable too?' he asked, strolling in behind her.

'What do you have?' she demanded tartly.

A brow arched. 'Just my birthday suit.'

'Then no, thank you.'

'Spoilsport!' he grinned, sitting down on the bed which rolled beneath his weight.

'I thought we were sleeping on the floor, so how come we were in bed this morning?' she asked, unfastening the scarf knotted around her hair.

His shoulders twitched in self-mockery. 'I decided I was being a louse when I saw you asleep down there, so I lifted you into bed and then ... then I guess I didn't feel like leaving. I must confess the water-bed isn't that bad.'

Judith unzipped her jeans, peeling them off. She could feel the shrewd assessment in his eyes as he followed every movement, and gradually she began to feel uneasy. Again there was this strange sensation of him being 'someone else'. Avoiding his look, she carefully folded the trousers and put them on a hanger in the wardrobe. She would not allow herself to be thrown into a state of confusion, she decided, steeling herself to his inspection. Unfastening the pearl buttons of her blouse, she shrugged it from her.

Time stood still. He was studying her gravely as though she represented some mathematical equation which hadn't produced the answer he had expected. 'Don't stop,' he murmured when she was stripped down to her white lace bra and briefs.

'Linc!' she protested.

Silently he rose from the bed and folded her into his arms. He was trembling. Linc never trembled, she thought in bewilderment, and a wave of tenderness swept over her. As he bent to kiss her brow she twined her arms around his neck, stroking his head, running her fingers through the thick dark hair. How could he be so familiar and yet so alien? He was gently kissing her eyelids, her nose, her lips. With increasing urgency his hands began to wander up and down her spine, caressing the silken skin, feeling the shape of her.

'Jude,' he whispered hoarsely, and then he plundered her mouth. He was a wild buccaneer, totally without mercy as he dragged her into his passion. His kiss was hungry, searching, forcing back her head, claiming her lips and yet, despite the onslaught, he was exciting her. The heat of the blood pounding below the surface of her skin had little to do with the tropical climate. Their mutual desire was clouding her brain.

His breathing was ragged as he unhooked her bra and tossed it blindly aside. 'Jude,' he murmured again, his voice thick with desire, 'you're superb.' There was a shaft of exquisite pleasure as he traced a circle around one tightening nipple with a long finger, and Judith threw back her head, moaning softly. Half-open, his mouth moved down her throat to her breasts, moistly kissing the swelling curves.

'No, Linc, no,' she pleaded as his hands slithered down her hips to rest on the tiny lace briefs. 'I might get pregnant. Wait, please wait.'

'I can't. I need you. I'm mad with wanting you. Jude! I've lain awake at nights for a whole year reliving the touch, the fragrance, the taste of you. You can't expect me to wait now.' His mouth returned to hers, claiming possession.

Palms against his chest, she forced herself from him. 'I don't want a baby.'

'Why not?' he demanded, searching for breath, taking deep shuddering gulps as he gained a measure of control.

She met the glitter of eyes sparking yellow with angry frustration. 'Not yet, perhaps in a year or so when the shop. . . .'

'The shop!' he spat in disgust. 'It's a bored housewife's plaything.'

Impotent rage began to swell inside her. 'I care about it,' she declared, raising her chin.

'Too much!' He took a threatening step towards her but, heart pounding like a tom-tom, she stood her ground; then, to her utter amazement, he smiled. 'Honey, if you could see yourself—chin tilted, breasts quivering with rage.' He pulled her back into his arms and laughed. It was the confident laugh of a man who always gets what he wants.

'No!' she cried, reeling from him. 'I don't want to make love.'

'Liar!' A grin tugged at the side of his mouth as he watched her, languidly stroking his beard.

Judith crossed her hands over her chest, shielding herself from his knowing inspection. 'I'm not making love unless you agree we won't have a child,' she declared rashly.

He raised a disdainful brow. 'Well, I'm sure as hell not prepared to take precautions, lady, so I guess it's back to celibacy.'

Her heart sank at his drawled response, but before she could say anything more there came a crunch of gravel on the drive and the sound of a vehicle slowing beneath the front porch.

'Wayne,' he declared, his nostrils flaring in derision. 'Come to rescue his damsel in distress, has he? I'll soon get rid of him.'

Ignoring the taunt, Judith gathered up her bra, quickly fastening it back into position. Through the open window came the sound of a car door slamming, footsteps, then the shrill of a feminine voice. Her eyes joined Linc's in mutual surprise, and his expression slumped so dramatically that she was filled with an hysterical desire to laugh, for horror and disbelief were equally mixed in his face.

'Magda!' he mouthed, and strode towards the door.

'I do enjoy visiting the Far East for a vacation,' Magda remarked, settling herself down on a canvas patio chair. 'But I wouldn't care to live here full time.'

Making no comment, Judith wheeled the striped sunbed out on to the lawn and reached for her tanning oil.

Magda's reconciliation scene with Linc had been a flamboyant display of tears and tragic gestures, as expected. Like the ham actress she was, she had milked the occasion dry and it had taken a full hour before normal life could be resumed. But despite her emotional state she had still managed to consume a hearty lunch and had then spent another hour unpacking her belongings and making herself at home in the spare room. Judith wondered how long her mother-in-law would stay this time before Linc's patience broke. Not too long, for judging by the look on his dark face as he sat beside Magda in the shade of the patio, his equilibrium was already sorely tried.

'I'll oil your back,' he offered, strolling out to join her in the sunshine.

She rolled on to her stomach. It would have been churlish to refuse his offer, but the rhythmic move- ment of his hands sliding over her bare skin was already sending flickers of desire through her. His fingers were so strong, so sure, so intimate that she was convinced he was deliberately arousing her, and

yet why? He had sounded as though he meant it when
he had said it was back to celibacy. Her heart fluttered.
He must have been teasing, for now he was massaging
her shoulders and her spine, the oiled fingers slithering
over the curves scarcely concealed by the tiny white
crochet bikini in an outright declaration of desire. For
an instant she was tempted to roll over on to her back,
drag him close and whisper 'Monkey Bay' into his ear.
He would know what she meant. . . .

'You're very tanned, Lincoln,' his mother called.
'Too much sun can be bad for you, it dries the
skin.'

His rhythm slowed, the strokes growing shorter.
'When there's a machine-gun trained on your back
and someone says get out there and dig, you don't
spend too much time worrying about your complexion.'

Magda's hand with its long manicured nails flew to
her mouth. 'My heavens! what were you digging?'

Linc straightened up, abruptly twisting the cap back
on to the bottle of suntan oil. 'Don't worry, not my own
grave, though it felt like it at times. We lived in a camp
in the middle of the jungle, and part of my duties was to
control the undergrowth and raise crops. I've become
an expert on tropical agriculture since I've been away,
and on forced labour.'

Deserting Judith, he prowled back to his chair,
collapsing into it, legs spread wide. Although she was
grateful that his hands were no longer following the
glistening contours of her body, perversely she missed
him. Laying her head on her hands, she studied him
from beneath her lashes. Perhaps the Che Guevara look
was attractive?

It was late afternoon, and although the sun was
sinking in the sky, it had lost none of its power to burn.
She would allow herself a quarter of an hour in its rays
and then move into the shade. Linc picked up a glass of

beer and as he raised it to his lips, his eyes met hers. Hastily she switched her attention to her mother-in-law. She was incredible. In her turquoise cotton dress, a matching headsquare tying back her dark hair, no-one would ever guess Magda had spent the previous twenty-four hours travelling across the world. She wasn't so helpless when it came down to brass tacks, Judith realised, for it must have taken quickfire organisation to have reserved a ticket, packed and closed up her house within hours of Linc's telephone call. Jet lag didn't appear to have touched her, for after a shower and change of clothes, Magda was as good as new, idly sipping a calorie-free cola and treating her son to a day-by-day account of what had happened to her since they last met. To *her*, Judith thought cynically, not to him.

Narrowing his eyes at the sun, Linc took another long swig of beer. He had resurrected an old pair of shorts from the back of a drawer, shorts which had been too tight in the old days, but which now fitted to perfection. Judith's eyes swung back to him. He fascinated her. It was remarkable how a hair-covered jaw and upper lip could transform a man.

'You've lost weight, Lincoln,' Magda announced, abandoning what sounded to be about day sixty-five, only three hundred more to go. She reached across and touched his arm. 'But you look very fit. I like a man to be fit. Cy is very fit for his age.'

'Who's Cy?' he asked.

With a waft of her lashes and a girlish giggle, Magda proceeded to give a detailed description of her latest beau, who appeared to have been in attendance for several months. 'He's in insurance. He had to fly to New York on business a few days ago, so when your call came through I decided to throw caution to the winds and rush out to see you.'

'And when does this Cy return?'

'In about ten days' time. I sent him a card with your address and telephone number. Who knows, he might decide to drop by when his business is finished.'

Judith trapped a scornful bubble of laughter. Nobody in his right mind would 'drop by' in Penang on the way from New York to Los Angeles, except perhaps her mother-in-law! Ten days, she realised, suddenly sitting upright on the lounger and crossing her legs—ten days of Magda! Her movement had been impatient, and strands of the hair she had twisted into a pile on top of her head sprang free. Sticking the pins into her mouth, she began fixing a fresh coil. The murmur of conversation resumed behind her; Magda had slid into gear once more. Over her shoulder, Judith flashed Linc a quick glance. He didn't seem to be listening to his mother. He was sprawled in his chair, eyes half-closed, legs stretched out before him, like some wild creature drowsing in the heat.

Ten days before her mother-in-law departed! Ten days, when she and Linc needed to be alone, working things out. There was a limit to how much of Magda she could stand, and in her present state of mind that limit was severely restricted. It was true that Magda had stayed for far longer in the past, but then Linc had been supportive, sharing her exasperation with his mother's foolish ways. It had been two against one, but already she knew he wasn't in the mood to be so helpful this time. Supposing he decided to return to flying immediately and demanded she act the gracious hostess? Would he expect her to neglect the shop merely to tour the island as Magda's sidekick? Her mother-in-law didn't want female companionship, she thought rebelliously. From past experience she knew that the minute an eligible man came into her sights Magda would virtually disown her. Blonde hair pinned back into place, she grumpily resumed her position on the sunbed.

'I had a reporter call me,' Magda gushed. 'I was leaving for the airport, so I promised to ring him as soon as I get back. He said he'd be very interested to hear my first-hand account of how you've survived the ordeal.' She readjusted the hemline of her dress across her knees. 'Naturally I explained how you have the right genes for dealing with such a crisis.'

'Don't you dare speak to the press about me,' Linc thundered, springing to his feet and towering over her, his whole body tense, the bunched muscles rock-hard beneath the gleaming teak of his skin.

Judith caught her breath. She had never seen him like this before, never known he possessed the power to intimidate so violently.

'You are not to say a single word to anyone about my life as a hostage—understand?' he snapped, his brows drawing together in black anger.

'Why . . . why, Lincoln!' his mother gasped, for once lost for words.

'What do you imagine the last year was—an adventure, some romantic episode?' he demanded brutally. 'It wasn't. It was dangerous and frightening and squalid. Can you realise the terror of living through each day wondering if those peasants might lose their temper over some trifling matter, and decide to fill you full of lead?' He wiped a hand across his brow. 'It was hell, and I don't want you on some stupid television programme or babbling to some reporter about your big brave son. I wasn't brave, I just lived each minute as it came, and as for your ridiculous fantasies about White Russians and my genes . . .' He swore loud and long.

Magda took a nervous sip of cola, her eyes darting everywhere but at her son. She was genuinely shocked by his attack and showed it. Judith realised today must be the first time Linc had openly condemned his mother's attitude, for in the past he had accepted her gossiping, her artificial swoops of mood, so long as they didn't

impinge too greatly on his world. With long-suffering
patience he had coped with her frivolous demands,
regarding her as a kind of fond joke whom fate had
foisted upon him. But it seemed he was no longer
prepared to be so amenable. His time as a hostage had
changed him in so many ways. Judith watched her
mother-in-law with anxious eyes. Her only sin was to be
foolish, and it seemed harsh of Linc to berate her in this
way. Magda looked bereft; she, too, was learning and
learning fast that the casual charmer of a year ago had
been replaced by a far different man.

Judith took pity. 'Would you like to drive down to
Wayne's house tomorrow, Magda? You've not seen the
baby yet and I know Esther's dying to show him off to
you. He's beautiful.'

'That would be nice,' Madga agreed in a subdued
voice. She cast a glance at Linc and gave an audible sigh
when she realised he had lounged back into his chair.
His anger seemed to have collapsed, for he was staring
up at the sky which was now filling with muted streaks
of pink and gold.

'Guess who I met the other day,' Magda said,
bouncing back.

'Who?' He treated her to a weary smile.

'Suzanne, she's freshly divorced.'

'How nice! First, second or third time?'

'Lincoln!' She dissolved into peals of relieved
laughter. The jokey Lincoln she knew of old, she could
cope with him though his humour did throw her
sometimes. 'Don't be dumb, Suzanne's been married
once and only for a few weeks.' Her tone hushed. 'I
heard a rumour it's never been properly consummated.'

'How about *im*properly?'

'Oh, *you*!' She was smiling now, back in her secure
world where she knew how far to tread. 'Suzanne
looked real cute. I always say there's no girls as cute
as Californian girls.'

'We all know what you say, Mother,' he remarked heavily.

'Present company excepted,' she added after a moment.

Judith produced a weak smile, and she almost wished she had never rescued Magda from Linc's fury. Her comments were plain unthinking, not malicious, but they irritated nonetheless.

Linc rose to his feet. 'Don't you think you should come out of the sun now, Jude? I'd hate that champagne colour of yours to turn into Campari. I'll move the sunbed for you.' He put down his beer and padded barefoot towards her.

All remnants of his anger had vanished, but there was still something in his manner which disturbed her. On the surface he was relaxed and convivial, but she sensed an inner distraction, an aloofness tinging the smile he gave her.

'Take my chair, I'll bring another,' he offered, folding the sunbed and resting it against the white-painted wall. Flowering periwinkles in pink and blue cascaded from glazed pots hung in macramé holders along one side of the tiled patio, and Judith plucked at a petal as she came into the shade. One day she must bring home some vases from Mr Lim's collection; they would make attractive containers for flowering shrubs. Sinking down into the chair, she wiped droplets of perspiration from her brow. Suddenly she was weary. She had forgotten how enervating the sun could be, for it was a long time since she had deserted the air-conditioned coolness of the shop to bask in the tropical heat. Linc positioned a chair beside her and stooped to lift his tankard.

'Look at that,' Magda shrieked, staring out wide-eyed at the lawn. Motionless, beneath a sprawling bougainvillaea, was a small reptile. Jumping to her feet, she clutched wildly at Linc's arm, making him spill his beer.

Judith laughed. 'It's only an iguana. They come into the garden from time to time, but they won't hurt you.'

The older woman was pale beneath her make-up. 'Are you sure?'

Linc steered her back into her chair. 'Relax, you're perfectly safe,' he assured her, laughing. He took a swig of beer, the froth white on his moustache before he brushed it away, and tossed a quick look at Judith. 'Most of the creatures in Penang are harmless, except the odd bird from foreign climes.'

The remark went straight over Magda's head. 'I don't know why you live out here, Lincoln. Surely you could operate a helicopter company in California?'

'I could. As a matter of fact I've been chewing the idea over in my mind.'

Judith's head snapped round, tendrils of blonde hair drifting freely about her cheeks. 'Since when?' she demanded.

'Since I spent twelve hellish months under armed guard in a sweltering tropical jungle,' he bit out.

Blue eyes like saucers, she stared at him. 'But . . . but you've not come to any decision?'

'Perhaps Suzanne's father would advance you a loan,' Magda interposed excitedly.

Linc twitched his nose. 'I hardly think so. I imagine that all he's heard about me being a mismatch of genes from White Russian princes and American frontiersmen would have cancelled out any reliability I may have had as a business proposition. Apart from the fact that doubtless you've kept everyone well informed of how I've spent the last year fighting tigers single-handed and swinging through trees,' he added drily.

He raised a hand as Magda started to protest her innocence. 'I don't need his cash. I expect Mr Cheng will buy up my share of the business here—he has first option. That will give me enough to start up in the States, and I reckon it's possible Mr Cheng might be willing to invest in me again. I intend to sound him out.'

'But the company here is doing so well,' Judith protested. 'Wayne went to look over two Fokkers; he intends to expand.'

Linc lifted a sarcastic brow. 'Wayne made a decision? You amaze me. I'd have bet money the company would have marked time while I've been away.'

'He hasn't actually signed on the dotted line yet, but he will,' she hedged, heartily wishing Wayne had shown more initiative.

'After he's spoken to me.'

'I expect so,' she agreed in a small voice, then her eyes began to spark with blue fire. 'I don't see why you want to leave now. You've always enjoyed life in the East.'

'I have,' he agreed. 'But there are limitations, restrictions on what you can do when you're in business as a foreigner. You must realise that from your dealings at the shop.'

'Yes, but we could easily stay on in Penang for a few more years and move to the States later, if necessary.'

He shrugged. 'What's the point? I've been out of touch for a year. It'll take months for me to settle back here, so I might as well devote the time to launching another company in the States. I had plenty of time for thinking while I was in captivity. I've thought it all through and I've worked everything out to the last detail, so everything should run smoothly.

To me this seems the perfect time for starting over.'

Judith gripped the wooden arms of her chair with taut fingers. 'Yes, to you it might seem perfect, but what about me? Where do I fit into the scheme of things?'

CHAPTER FIVE

A CHAIR leg scraped across the tiles as he rose to his feet. 'I had presumed you would come with me,' he replied, fixing her with cool brown eyes.

His use of the past tense speared Judith's heart like a lance, and she stared at him in dismay.

'A woman's place is by her husband's side,' Magda chimed in righteously.

Linc flashed her a look of pure exasperation. 'It was a long flight and I'm sure you must be worn out. Wouldn't you like to go to your room and take a nap before dinner?'

'No, thanks. I met this English guy on the plane, he was a real gentleman.' She chortled with careless delight at the memory, placing her hand on Judith's arm to claim her attention. 'You know the type, so well-dressed and his manners—wow! I wouldn't be surprised if he was a lord travelling incognito. We started chatting and . . .'

'Get to the point,' Linc growled, tipping back his head and draining the tankard with one almighty gulp.

Magda shot him a wary glance. 'And he gave me some pills, so I slept and I don't feel tired, but I'll go and rest as soon as I do,' she yapped in conclusion.

He let out a breath of open annoyance and, with a touch of malice, Judith decided that this was the rare occasion when she sided with her mother-in-law. 'I think you'd be wise to stay awake until bedtime,' she smiled solicitously. 'If you sleep now, chances are you'll spend the night tossing and turning.'

With a grunt of derision Linc strode away towards the kitchen to refill his glass.

'Suzanne'll be so pleased to hear Lincoln is moving back to the States,' Magda prattled on thoughtlessly. 'She wanted to know all about him when we last met.'

'Oh yes?' Wearily Judith pushed the hair from her brow. Her skin was tingling with the sun and her head starting to throb. She was in no mood to listen to tales of Linc's old girlfriends. What she needed was time alone with him, time to talk things over. Her mind buzzed with questions. Did he really mean to cut their ties with Penang? Did he really intend to keep away from her unless she agreed to have a child? She accepted that previously he had made the decisions in their marriage, but he had always considered her. He had never ridden roughshod over her feelings, as he appeared to be doing now.

'Suzanne's a lovely girl, and you should see her apartment! It's large enough to house a battalion, though naturally she's living there alone now. Such a shame.'

Judith tried to wring out a drop of enthusiasm. 'Do you go there often?'

'I've never been personally,' her mother-in-law confessed with a giggle. 'A friend of a friend was at one of Suzanne's parties and she filled me in. We spent a whole morning discussing the apartment. A famous interior decorator from Beverly Hills fixed it up. There's a jacuzzi and a sauna, leather drapes and real gold faucets, the lights work by remote control, the telephones are carved onyx and I believe she has a mirrored ceiling in her bedroom.'

'Sounds like heaven on earth,' Linc commented wryly as he dropped back down into his chair.

Magda hesitated, struggling to decide whether she could detect a trace of sarcasm, but when he threw her a cheerful smile she discarded her suspicions and continued the tale, droning on to give a blow-by-blow description of each room. 'You could live in an apartment like that when you come back to L.A.,' she finished triumphantly.

'I doubt it. I don't consider mirrored ceilings are quite my style,' he remarked. 'In any case I won't be based in L.A. I've decided to work out of San Francisco.'

'What! Why?' Magda wailed.

'Because I prefer San Francisco,' he said, the words sounding as though they were nails and he was hammering each one in separately. 'There's a wider opening for tourist trade and I already have several contacts in the area.'

The fact he was using the first person singular brought a chill to Judith's heart, and his plans were becoming to sound more and more like concrete facts with every word.

'What's the time scale for this move of yours?' she demanded, tapping an irritated tattoo on the arm of her chair. In the past they would never have discussed private matters when her mother-in-law was around, and it did go against the grain, but questions were chewing at her mind, urgently needing satisfaction.

A large shoulder heaved. 'As quickly as possible, two or three months, I guess.'

'A hit and run operation?'

'If you like.'

She was beginning to see red as conflicting emotions warred for supremacy within her. What should she do? Meekly comply with his plans as she would have done twelve months ago, relying on Linc to know best, or force him to realise she was now an independent spirit with other considerations apart from him?

'But it's not what *I* like, is it?'

The projected location surprised and dismayed her. San Francisco was a beautiful city, but they had always maintained they would live as far from Magda as possible.

'I had no way of knowing you had taken over Mandarin Antiques,' he said patiently, as though she was a fractious child. 'Naturally that alters the scenario somewhat.'

'Thank you.' Her words dripped vitriol. 'I appear to have scored a point at last.'

'Don't turn this into a battle, Jude. As far as I'm concerned there's nothing to fight over.'

'*Exactly!* You consider my agreement is a foregone conclusion.'

'California's a great place to settle,' Magda intruded. 'Even San Fran.'

Hair tumbling in agitation, Judith spun to face her. 'I'm sure it is, but right now *I* want to stay in Penang!'

'Do you?' Incredulity drew her plucked brows closer. 'I can't think why.'

With taut fingers Judith stabbed the fallen curls of hair back into her topknot, pinning them into place. Lord! she wanted to scream. Scream at the silly woman on one side of her and the arrogant male sprawled on the other. She swivelled to Linc, chest heaving with fury as another question popped into her head. 'And what happens if Wayne decides to follow you to the States and the company here folds?' she slammed.

Linc's eyes were hooded; he seemed mesmerised by the rise and fall of her breasts beneath the scraps of white crochet. Breasts which were smooth and round. He licked his lips, his mouth quirking as he at last forced his gaze up to hers, and Judith was filled with the urgent need to slap his face for him. She glowered back, defying the amused desire which was dimpling the slashes on his cheeks. If his mother hadn't been there she would have told him exactly what he could do with his sexy looks.

'There's no room in my plans for Wayne,' he informed her smoothly. 'He's a big boy now and it's unhealthy for him to hitch himself to my star forever.'

She frowned. 'You don't need to worry your pretty little head about him,' he jibed, the yellow flecks in his eyes shining bright in the glow from the setting sun. 'He has an excellent track record in flying, he's dependable and his personal attributes are such that everyone likes him . . . and trusts him,' he added heavily.

'He has a cute smile,' Magda murmured in the background.

'He's not innovative and he's not ambitious,' Linc continued as though she had never spoken. 'But Mr Cheng has a high regard for him and the past year has proved he is capable of looking after the business.' His voice dropped to a throaty growl. 'And my wife.'

She stared at him coldly. 'Wayne is patient and understanding,' she began.

'And he always does exactly what you want him to do,' Linc countered. 'High calibre compliance, that's his stock-in-trade.'

'There are some real snazzy places to visit around San Francisco.' Magda's voice drifted into the conversation like a feather into a blast furnace.

'He's considerate,' Judith continued doggedly. 'And never moody and . . . and he's helped me a lot over the past year.'

'Lay off it, you'll be wanting to give him a sainthood next,' Linc drawled.

'Do you think the Government will award you a medal, Lincoln?' his mother asked.

In reply came a bark of incredulous laughter. 'Jeez!' he said, shaking his head.

With one fluid movement Judith propelled herself out of her chair. 'I'm going to take a shower,' she informed them and marched away into the bungalow.

Ten minutes later, as she was stepping from beneath the water, Linc came in. For a moment he rested a shoulder against the door jamb and watched, his brown eyes licking over her dripping body. The emotion in his look disturbed her and she grabbed a towel and twisted it rapidly around her, securing it beneath her armpits.

'Mr Cheng has been on the telephone,' he told her, smiling at the prim action. 'He's invited us to dinner at the penthouse this evening—apparently Kee-Ann has been pestering him. As you were busy I risked your wrath and made a decision without consultation. I said we'd go, is that okay, ma'am?' He gave a low mocking bow.

'Yes, it is.' She kept her voice even, for the shower had washed away the white-hot blaze of her anger and now, in a calmer frame of mind, she saw that she must try to be less emotional. 'Is Magda going too?'

He nodded, straightening up. 'I know she's a pain, but we can't desert her on her first evening here, even if she did arrive uninvited. As she strongly denies the possibility she could be tired, I was forced to ask Mr Cheng if we could take her along, and, of course, he was delighted. She's rushed off to her room to change and re-do her warpaint!' A brow arched. 'I hope I have her stamina when I'm in my fifties.'

'You will,' she said flatly, padding past him.

'Do you know whether the tailor's shop in the arcade is likely to be open now?' he asked. 'I need something to wear this evening. Tee shirt and jeans seem a little unorthodox for dining out Cheng-style.'

Judith allowed herself a small smile. Mr Cheng's world was one of luxurious conservatism. Whenever she met him, either in the controlled cool of the Sentosa Country Club or beneath the searing heat of the tropical sun, he was inevitably wearing a dark three-piece business suit and a crisp white shirt. She lifted her watch. 'They're due to close in ten minutes' time. Shall I give Mr Nair a ring and tell him you're on your way? I'm sure he'll be happy to wait if I ask him. He'd never willingly turn down the opportunity to make an extra dollar.'

Hurriedly Linc dragged on his tee shirt. 'Please.' On his way out of the door he paused. 'I can see there are certain advantages to having a wife "in the trade",' he smiled.

Judith went out into the living-room and dialled the number. Mr Nair was only too happy to agree and she felt pleasantly smug as she returned to the bedroom to pat herself dry. Linc wasn't the only one who could control events, if necessary. She closed the shutters and switched on the air-conditioning. Within minutes the machine had flooded the room with cool air and the temperature began to fall. She relaxed as the tension faded from her. Perhaps she had lain too long in the sun and that was what had prompted her anger to boil over so alarmingly? Now, thank goodness, she felt much calmer. Losing her temper with Linc was a waste of time, she should have known that from the past. Instead she must handle the situation with calm control. Follow his example, in other words. Previously they had always talked things through, so why not now?

When she was dry she raked through her wardrobe, settling on a stylish silk-chiffon top with matching harem pants. The outfit was in a delicate shade of oyster, with a wide gold leather belt which emphasized her slender waist. As the top was skimpy, she fastened a wide gold choker around her neck and wore three gold bangles on one upper arm. She was brushing a shimmer of pinky-bronze shadow on her eyelids when Linc returned.

'The stock that Nair guy carries is unbelievable,' he said, slinging a couple of plastic carrier bags on to the bed. 'He was telling me about his twenty-four-hour tailoring service. I think next week I'll go along and be measured up for some shirts and slacks.'

Judith opened her eyes wide and began to wield her mascara wand. 'He's very popular with the tourists,' she remarked, but as she caught a glimpse of him through the mirror, her hand faltered. She swung round. 'You've had your hair cut!'

He grinned, running his hand over the back of his head. The unruly locks had gone, and now his hair was thickly shaped to the nape of his neck, the glossy beard trimmed to respectability. 'The barber's was open, so. . . .'

'It looks much better, more like the old Linc,' she smiled, returning to her make-up.

He stepped behind her and rested his hands on her shoulders, his touch firm and warm. 'But I'm not the old Linc,' he said quietly, and it sounded like a warning. He gave a sudden shiver. 'It's like a fridge in here, must we have the air-con running?'

'If we don't there'll be sweaty patches on your shirt before you even hit the front door,' she warned.

He made for the bathroom. 'You're right, you win.'

She completed her make-up and twisted her hair into a classical pleat at the back of her head, fastening it with gold pins studded with mother-of-pearl. She slipped her feet into high gold leather sandals and added a final dab of perfume to her pulse points.

'You smell good,' Linc commented, wandering back into the room half-clad. 'Je Reviens, right?' He bent his head, burying his face in her neck and she felt his lips part. As his tongue darted out to lick her skin, she quivered and the familiar feeling of desire swelled as his grip tightened on her shoulders.

'You shouldn't do this to me, Jude,' he muttered.

'Do what?' she questioned, feigning ignorance of the emotion lapping over the two of them.

'Be so damned beautiful.' He sounded almost angry. Impatiently he released her and went to the bed, taking out cream slacks and a chocolate-brown shirt from one of the plastic bags.

We're tormenting each other, she thought unhappily as she watched him dress. Linc was so virile, brimming with such powerful masculinity that she almost swayed with desire as her body cried out to his. The aching need was denied as she turned away to fiddle aimlessly with the clasp of her purse.

He buckled his belt, combed his hair, then turned and grinned. 'Come on, honey,' he said, holding out a hand.

'I guess this is what's classed as a fun car?' Magda asked, her eyes wandering uneasily over the confined interior of the Mini.

From the back seat Judith saw Linc smother a grin, and she bristled. 'It's reliable,' she defended, and was tempted to add that it would seem twice as roomy if her husband wasn't filling half the available space with his massive shoulders.

'Like Wayne,' he jibed so quietly that she doubted whether Magda, sitting beside him, would have heard.

Judith had scrambled into the rear seat, pushing aside a motley collection of tissue paper and discarded wrappings which she had been meaning to clear for weeks. It would have been unfair to expect the older woman to have risked crushing her finery in the restricted space.

Magda looked like a million dollars, albeit in used notes, but still a dazzling apparition for all that. Her full-length dress was a riot of rainbow shades, the bodice and skirt each ending in jagged handkerchief points which drifted becomingly as she moved. With painstaking expertise her dark hair had been arranged into a leonine torrent of curls, and her make-up was dramatic—prune eyeshadow, the usual spiky lashes, thick black eyeliner and a coating of plummy lipstick.

Resisting the temptation to bite back at Linc, Judith ignored him. 'You look stunning tonight, Magda,' she smiled. 'Mr Cheng will be complimenting you on your appearance again.'

'Thanks, honey. He's always had a soft spot for me.'

It was true. The dapper Chinese was fascinated by Magda's flamboyance, and, surprisingly, a firm friendship had sprung up between them, beneath the ever-watchful eye of Mrs Cheng.

When they arrived at the Country Club they took the private lift and within seconds were whisked up to the tenth floor. 'Welcome, welcome,' Mr Cheng beamed, as a servant ushered them into a vast lounge. The room was richly furnished with straightbacked crimson couches, dark antique furniture and oriental rugs. Dramatic displays of ancient Chinese weapons were stark against plain white walls, and huge porcelain vases on pedestals jostled for position with tubs of lavish greenery. One wall was made entirely of glass, and the sliding panels had been pushed aside to open out on to a wide balcony where the evening breeze whispered through banks of bright blossoms. Mrs Cheng, Kee-Ann and two of her older brothers were waiting, and after Mr Cheng's fulsome greetings they, too, offered a welcome with smiles and a formal shaking of cool hands.

'Isn't this wonderful?' Mr Cheng remarked, sitting down beside Judith on a brocade couch. 'Both of them have returned home safe and sound.' He cast a fond glance to where Linc and Kee-Ann were talking together on the balcony.

Drinks had been served by a smiling manservant and now everyone had split up into groups. Magda was recounting some garrulous anecdote to one of the Cheng sons, while Mrs Cheng and the other boy were examining a tall cabinet in a far corner of the room. Judith's eyes shone in anticipation. It was a new addition; Mr Cheng was an ardent collector of antiques himself, and she knew the cabinet would have a fascinating history. She longed to take a closer look. Later, she promised herself as her host continued.

'Kee-Ann is full of praise for your husband. She can't

speak too highly of his care during that troubled period.' Mr Cheng pursed his lips. 'She must have been a great responsibility. My daughter tends to be a little wayward at times.'

'She doesn't look wayward,' Judith protested gently. Indeed in her navy dress with its white collar of broderie anglaise, Kee-Ann was the epitome of the well-brought-up child, neat and biddable. But suddenly she laughed, and Judith's heart missed a beat. The Chinese girl had thrown back her head, sending the wings of raven-black hair swirling, and there was a brief glimpse of a more sophisticated creature. For a second she rested her hand on Linc's arm, but then, as if sensing onlookers, she removed it quickly. Judith wondered if Mr Cheng had noticed the intimate gesture. She had never known the girl well, and indeed now she wondered if she had ever known her at all!

'It would have been far easier for Linc if he had been alone when he was captured, then he could have attempted to escape,' her host mused. 'I fear Kee-Ann's presence was a liability. A man can exist on the run, he can survive, but the prospect of risking another person's life is inhibiting, especially a pampered young girl. How could he subject her to the dangers of the jungle?' He sighed. 'She was a very wicked child, forcing herself on him like that.'

Judith's brows lifted in puzzlement. 'Surely it was you who arranged for Linc to take Kee-Ann with him when he drove up to Songkhla? Wasn't she going up to stay with a girlfriend for a short holiday?'

'She had been invited,' Mr Cheng agreed, 'but no date had been fixed. It was only when she discovered Linc was having to motor up into Thailand that impulsively she decided she must go. You know what these young girls are like; it had to be then and there. I pointed out that the journey could be dangerous, there had been recent skirmishes with the Communists in the

border country, but she refused to take no for an
answer. That's what I mean about her being wayward.
Since she's lived in America she has become a little too
self-willed.'

Judith's thoughts trekked back a year. One of the
helicopter pilots had been smitten with a virus after
delivering some holiday-makers to Songkhla, a seaside
resort in southern Thailand. He had been too ill to fly
home immediately, and as bookings were heavy there
was no way a chopper could be allowed to remain out
of action. There had been no alternative but for Linc to
hire a car and motor the long journey north in order to
collect the aircraft and the sickly pilot. It was while he
and Kee-Ann had been travelling along the jungle road
that insurgents had swooped. Distractedly she fingered
the choker at her neck. Until now she had always
presumed it was at Mr Cheng's request that Linc had
agreed to deliver Kee-Ann to her friend's house at
Songkhla. Vaguely she recalled Ah Fong's words—
'That one bad girl.'

'Linc reminds me of a pirate with his beard,' Mr
Cheng smiled, breaking into her thoughts. 'All he needs
are two golden earrings to complete the illusion.'

'And a cutlass in his hand,' she responded, silently
adding, so he can swashbuckle his way through,
chopping down the opposition without a care.

Magda had tired of the Cheng son, or perhaps it was
the other way around, and was now bearing down,
arms outstretched. Mr Cheng leapt quickly to his feet as
if to deflect the first impact of her embrace, but allowed
her to kiss his cheek. Judith hid a grin. Her host was so
conservative, it was against his code of conduct to show
any affection in public, and she doubted that even Mrs
Cheng would dare to go so far. Her mother-in-law,
however, was gloriously immune to such reservations
and eagerly pushed her host back on to the couch and
sat beside him, her arm linking his. Mr Cheng smiled

uneasily, as though he realised he shouldn't strictly be enjoying Magda's attentions, but he was.

'You must be a proud woman,' he said, nodding towards Linc.

'I certainly am. He's one of the chosen few.'

Mr Cheng's face clouded. 'I'm afraid I don't understand.'

After a hasty glance around the room, she leaned furtively towards him. 'He's sworn me to silence, but naturally I wonder just what information it was he passed on to those secret service agents in Thailand!'

Judith giggled. 'Magda! You know he told you that the gang who held him were politically nondescript.'

Bosom swelling with importance, Magda pulled herself upright. 'You never know. Lincoln was ultra-insistent I say nothing to the media, so there must be a very good reason.'

Linc wandered over. 'You're not fantasising again, are you, Mother?' he drawled.

She was staunchly denying it when Mrs Cheng announced that dinner was ready.

The meal was delicious, eight courses of Chinese cuisine in the Cantonese style, ranging from the delicate flavour of steamed pomfret with bamboo shoots, to the richness of sweet and sour pork. Judith made small talk with the Cheng sons who were seated on either side, and determinedly left all notions of Kee-Ann's waywardness for later. Why waste time worrying about some mere pinprick of unease when the company and the food were excellent?

'It's great to be back in civilization once more, isn't it?' Linc asked Kee-Ann as everyone rose and made their way back into the lounge for coffee and liqueurs.

Judith's brows drew together. There was some hidden inflection in his words, something she was unable to translate. With steady blue eyes she watched the pair of them. Kee-Ann had paused and was gazing up at Linc, silently sending him a message. Icy claws began to scratch at Judith's heart.

'I'm sure you must be longing to take a look at my new cabinet,' Mr Cheng said, coming beside her.

'Yes, yes please,' she stammered, turning to him with a bright smile, but try as she might it was impossible to find the right degree of enthusiasm for the cabinet. Although it was an authenticated piece of great age, beautifully carved, her mind was numb to its interest. All she could think about was Linc and Kee-Ann, living together in captivity for almost a year.

With what she hoped were discreet glances, she noted that Linc was now talking to Mrs Cheng on the balcony while Kee-Ann listened meekly to Magda's tales. Without meaning to be, she found herself on guard, watching them both. From time to time Linc would glance across at the girl, his dark eyes sombre, his mouth grim.

'So if you should come across its partner any time,' Mr Cheng was saying, 'I'd be grateful if you would put me in touch.'

She looked at him blankly.

'They come in pairs,' he explained. 'You know—two.'

'Oh yes, yes. I'll certainly bear that in mind.' She knew she was floundering, but Kee-Ann had left Magda and was walking across the lounge towards her.

'I know you're interested in jade, Mrs Cassidy,' the girl said in her soft light voice as she joined them. 'I have a collection in my room. Perhaps you would like to see it?'

For the first time in her life Judith felt like an Amazon. Although she was only five foot four, she towered above the Chinese girl, and as she looked down at the willow-slim figure, the narrow shoulders, she became awkward by comparison. Kee-Ann was a doll, a porcelain doll.

Cool white fingers touched her bare arm. 'Do come and see,' the girl persisted, and the gentle pressure seemed to take on the cold clamp of talons.

'I don't know much about jade, it's not really in my range of interest,' she protested as the girl steered her through a corridor and into a pretty pink and white bedroom.

Kee-Ann closed the door firmly. 'That doesn't matter,' she said. 'I really want to speak to you about something else.'

She walked over to the window and stood for a moment, gazing out at the beach far below them. Judith joined her. In the moonlight she could make out the white curl of waves as they rolled over the sand. The ocean stretched out like a black quilt, and it was impossible to discover where the sea separated from the sky.

'Before I speak I must insist on your secrecy,' the girl said in a clear, level tone. 'What is said in this room must go no further.'

'But . . .?' she began, with an icy premonition that something disastrous was about to be revealed.

'Can I rely on that, Mrs Cassidy?' Kee-Ann demanded.

Judith spread her hands in bewilderment. 'Yes, of course, but. . . .'

'I need your help. You see, there's a possibility I may be pregnant.'

Judith gasped. She felt as though someone had kicked her hard in the stomach, and it was all she could do not to bend double and moan aloud. Her mind lurched drunkenly. Had Kee-Ann been forced to submit at gunpoint to one of the Communists? No, Linc had said they were not evil men, just unintelligent for the most part. If they had raped the Chinese girl he would have been bound to tell her. Her head began to swim. It seemed far more likely that it had been Linc who was

Kee-Ann's lover—who else could it be? Trumpets blared loud and discordant in her temples. Linc and Kee-Ann! How could she have been so blind as not to see the signs? He had told her they had become close, but not this close, she pleaded inwardly. 'Why are you telling me?' she protested.

'You are the only one I can turn to.'

In confusion, Judith stared at her. Kee-Ann's detachment was remarkable. Her poise had never faltered and the black almond-shaped eyes which met hers showed no trace of anguish.

'If I am pregnant I will need to have an abortion,' she continued matter-of-factly. 'If I were in the States it would be simple to arrange, but here . . .' she waved a graceful hand, 'here on the island discretion is vital. My family must never know. The Chinese are not so . . . so advanced, is that the right word? as Westerners. If my father found out I would bring disgrace to our family name, it would be a tremendous loss of face. If I approach an Asian doctor he would report back to my father immediately, so that is out of the question.' She turned to the window, gazing out at the night. 'My mother told me you had miscarried, Mrs Cassidy, and that you had been taken to the private hospital here which expatriates use. I understand there are several European doctors on the staff. I would be grateful if you would put me in touch with one who will be sympathetic towards my case.'

There were beads of perspiration on Judith's brow, she had broken out into a cold sweat. As she watched the girl her nerves leapt erratically. Her calm composure seemed almost an insult. Here she was, asking for help from the wife of her—Judith's heart froze—her lover, and apparently feeling not a single pang of remorse.

'Does . . . does Linc know about this?' she gulped.

Kee-Ann shook her head. 'No. I don't want to upset him, he's been so very good to me.'

Bile rose in her throat. 'I think he should be told. After all it's, it's . . .' The words refused to come out. It's his child, she thought despairingly. She had lost his first baby and now this cold, calculating creature was intent on destroying the second. 'I'll tell him if you won't,' she determined as her fingernails cut deep into her palms. 'It's only right he should be made aware of what's happening.'

'*No!*' At last Kee-Ann's composure cracked and the workings of the small hands clasped tightly at her waist revealed a measure of human frailty. 'He mustn't be involved. I cannot repay his kindness by flinging this . . . this calamity at him.' The pale hands grew still. 'I do not know for certain yet if I *am* pregnant. I have been under so much strain that there is still room for doubt, you understand?'

Judith took a deep breath. 'I understand, but if there is a child you must tell him. He'll . . . he'll help you.'

Decisively the girl shook her head. 'Linc must never know. I am adamant that I shall have an abortion and I can't risk him trying to change my mind. You know how fond he is of children, Mrs Cassidy. When we were held captive he told me many times how much he hoped you were already carrying his child. I'm sure it was a great disappointment for him when he discovered it was not to be.' She shook her head again. 'Linc must not be involved. It's my body, my destiny, and I can't afford to have him bringing pressure to bear. I have my future to consider. I'm not boasting when I tell you I have a quick brain and a grasp of realities. I'm a straight A student. My father intends me to play a leading role in his business empire one day and that is my wish also. A child at this stage in my life would be a catastrophe.' She took a step forward. 'I realise the news must be something of a shock. I don't require any action from you right now, but I would be grateful if you would consider my request. I like to be prepared. If you could provide the name of a European gynaecologist within the next week or so, I would be eternally grateful.' She lifted her narrow shoulders into a gesture of resignation. 'On the other hand, if you should not feel willing to help, then I intend to make some excuse to my family and fly to the States.'

'So you intend to . . . to dispose of the baby, if there is a baby, come what may?'

'I do.' The answer was final.

Judith rubbed her forehead in agitation. 'To be honest, I don't know what to do.'

The cool fingers touched her arm. 'Think it over, Mrs Cassidy. Now, shall we join the others?'

In a fog of confusion Judith followed the girl back into the lounge. Everyone else had moved out on to the balcony where the air was a little cooler, but Kee-Ann paused and began to discuss the jade collection they had never examined. What a remarkable character she was! The present delaying tactics were to allow her victim to recover—for victim she was, albeit an innocent one. As the girl chattered, Judith's eyes were drawn to Linc. He was standing with Mrs Cheng, a brandy goblet loosely clasped in one hand, his dark head bent attentively as he listened. His hostess must have reached the punchline, for he smiled, his teeth gleaming white against the thickness of beard and tanned skin. The change in his physical appearance hit her again. Yes, he *was* a stranger, and in more ways than one. A year ago she would never have believed he would have been unfaithful to her, but now . . .

There was no denying the fact that with or without the beard he was an attractive and sensual male. She was well aware that his past was dotted with affairs with women collected piecemeal as he had flown his jets around the world. On many occasions Magda had waxed loud and long about all the wealthy, wonderful women her son could have married, but didn't.

Miserably she twisted her wedding ring around her finger. But she had also been convinced that Linc was a man who kept his word. When he had repeated their marriage vows he had meant what he said, that he would be true to her only. Her mind see-sawed. Perhaps one of the guards had forced his attentions on Kee-Ann without Linc's knowledge. There was a blissful moment of relief, but then, as she thought it through, she realised it was highly improbable. They had lived in close proximity in the jungle, so surely if Kee-Ann had disappeared for any length of time Linc would have been alert to the fact and questioned her? She might be a cool customer now, but her behaviour as a hostage must have been far less assured. No way would she have been able to deceive Linc if she had been attacked.

With a flash of insight, Judith saw it all—a man caring for a frightened, beautiful girl, surrounded by enemies and in constant fear of death. Kee-Ann would have clung to Linc for support as she had clung to Wayne. She rubbed her knuckles against her chin in a gesture of despair. How could she condemn them? Wouldn't she have reacted in a similar way? Wouldn't she have been desperate for the comfort of a man's arms? Her heart plunged as she realised that the slide into making love would have been so natural.

A waiter was passing by. 'Could I have a brandy, please? A large one.' When he returned she took a swift gulp and it poured down her throat like liquid fire, making her splutter.

Kee-Ann smiled, waiting for her to recover, then she took hold of her elbow and steered her forward. 'Shall we go and join the others on the balcony?' She gave a little laugh. 'You must be wondering how I managed to keep my skin so pale when Linc is burnt dark brown?'

Judith frowned. That was one topic she had not got around to dealing with but, yes, she supposed it was rather odd.

The girl laughed again, a high tinkling sound. 'The truth is I spent most of my time inside the hut reading.'

'Reading?'

'I suspect that Sumphote, the leader of the group, initially intended to subvert me. He kept me supplied with literature, and every time he went home to his village, wherever that was, he returned with a huge pile of reading matter.' She giggled like a mischievous child. 'After a while he realised that political theses are not my style and then he provided the classics and some paperback novels. He was very kind to me.'

'Who was?' a deep voice asked. Linc had joined them.

Kee-Ann lowered her eyes, the dark lashes fanning discreetly on the porcelain-pale cheeks. 'Sumphote,' she whispered.

A muscle tightened in his jaw. 'Sumphote and company are in jail now, and the sooner you forget about them the better.'

'Yes, Linc,' she agreed, all milk and honey. The iron-willed young woman of a few minutes ago had been replaced by the demure Miss Cheng.

Judith took another sip of brandy. Her thoughts were splintered, each with its own needle-sharp point ready to stab into her heart.

'The conversation must have been real interesting,' Linc teased, his eyes flicking between the two girls. 'You've been gone ages.' He slipped his arm around Judith's waist and pulled her close against him. Instinctively, needing comfort, she rested her head against his shoulder. 'I missed you,' he murmured into her ear.

Mr Cheng had now joined them and he stood for a moment, smiling benignly at the sight of Judith and Linc together. 'I must congratulate you on your decorum over the past twelve months, Judith,' he smiled. 'What self-control! What composure! I'm full of admiration.' His shiny black eyes turned to Linc. 'She was an example to us all. Many times I left my wife in tears, but when I went down to see Judith in her shop she was the model of propriety, quietly going about her day's work as though nothing had happened.'

His words made Judith squirm.

'Indeed!' Linc said, his arm falling from her waist.

'No fuss, no hysterics,' Mr Cheng continued, gathering deadly momentum. 'Magda was absolutely distraught, but your wife handled the calamity with superb control. Naturally Wayne was supportive, but I really feel she has the inner strength to weather any storm alone.'

Judith stared down into her glass. What was intended as praise had sounded to her ears like a condemnation, an account of how little she had missed Linc. Uneasily she glanced at him and was not surprised to discover that his reaction appeared to be identical to hers. He had shoved one hand into his trouser pocket and was taking a slow, thoughtful slug of brandy, his dark eyes impassive. If only she could read what was lurking in those brown depths. One thing was certain; whatever it was, it wasn't delight at her demeanour as a hostage widow. There was an awkward lull in the conversation, and desperately she wanted him to say something, anything.

'I think it's time we went home,' was what he did say, turning his hair-sprinkled wrist to inspect his watch.

There was a leaden feeling in her stomach as she followed his example and carefully thanked her host and hostess for a pleasant evening.

'You'll consider what we discussed?' Kee-Ann murmured as they said farewell.

'Yes,' she promised helplessly. How could she do otherwise when the girl's revelation had turned her life inside out and upside down?

For once Magda's meaningless chatter was balm as it clouded around her like cotton wool, eradicating any need for her to open her mouth on the way home. Magda said everything—how cute Kee-Ann had looked, how cute the Cheng boys were, what a cute apartment Mr and Mrs Cheng owned. Linc was silent, too, and it was only when Magda had kissed them both a lipsticked goodnight and flown to her room like some brilliant dragonfly, that there was any need for words.

'Did Kee-Ann say much about our experiences with the Communists?' Linc asked as he climbed into bed beside her.

Judith pulled the sheet up to her chin. 'Not really.' She stared at the ceiling; no, she hadn't imagined it, he *did* sound wary. She turned her head on the pillow and looked across. His eyes were closed. 'Did you expect her to reveal something . . . er . . . something exciting?' she asked and felt her palms moisten with nervous perspiration.

There was silence. For a moment she wondered if he had fallen asleep, but then his eyes opened and it was his turn to examine the ceiling. 'Kee-Ann only reveals those things she wants to reveal,' he said mysteriously. He reached across and his lips brushed hers. 'Goodnight, see you in the morning.'

CHAPTER SIX

JUDITH awoke slowly, struggling up through a quagmire of unease, not quite knowing why she should be unhappy, only that she was. Then her blue eyes sprang open wide and all the upheaval of yesterday evening hammered itself back into her mind. When she turned her head, it was to discover that the bed beside her was empty. Linc had gone, and she didn't know whether to be relieved or disappointed. Wrapping the sheet around her, she curled up into a self-protective ball and felt the pit of her stomach cramp with pain. What should she do now? What *could* she do? Not much, though perhaps, just perhaps, Linc wasn't the father of Kee-Ann's child. Be realistic, she warned herself, all the facts point to that conclusion. A sigh of despair escaped her lips. She had promised Kee-Ann she would keep their conversation a secret, and in any case she refused to act the outraged wife and fling his adultery in his face; she loved him too much to do that—loved him too much and understood too well.

As she examined the situation she began to feel calmer. Love appeared to play no part in the girl's saga, her only concern was to ensure there would be no disruption of her planned life, and Linc wasn't a part of that plan. If this proved to be a false alarm, then the present distress was a hiccup, though an appalling one, but Judith realised she must force herself to dismiss the memory of what had taken place in the jungle for what it was—an understandable lapse which had no real meaning in the context of her marriage. But if there *was* a baby. . . .

She resolved to face up to that problem later. For the

moment she must take life one step at a time, it was the only way. Suddenly Mandarin Antiques didn't seem so important any longer.

'Hi, sleepyhead.' Linc prowled into the room and as she watched him flinging wide the wooden shutters her pulses broke into a canter. The lean, muscled physique had lost none of its power to arouse her and she longed to be held close in his arms. Her mouth faltered into a shaky smile as she pushed aside the haunting shades of doubt. No, he hadn't broken their marriage vows, surely another man must be responsible for the Chinese girl's dilemma?

Returning her smile, he lifted a droll brow. 'I'm the only person with any energy in this joint. Magda's door is firmly closed and you were snoring when I left.'

'I don't snore!' she protested, narrowing her eyes at him. 'Where have you been? You look disgustingly bright-eyed and bushy-tailed.'

He sat down on the edge of the bed beside her. 'I've been to the pad to have a quick refresher course on what's been happening in the helicopter world. A couple of the mechanics were there, so they started putting me in the picture.'

'But we're seeing Wayne later today; he'll bring you up to date,' she replied, vexed at the way he seemed determined to belittle his cousin. 'We said we'd drive down with Magda to visit him.'

'That was your idea.'

Linc was regarding her with sombre brown eyes and he stretched out a tanned finger, idly dragging it across one naked shoulder, over the base of her throat, to the other shoulder. The grave emotion in his look unsettled her. For a fleeting second he seemed lost, and she was filled with a need to comfort him, or was it that she needed to comfort herself? She didn't wait to analyse the feeling.

'Don't I get a good-morning kiss!' she pouted as the finger retraced its journey. He was unsmiling as he bent to deposit a brief kiss on her cheek. 'You can do better than that,' she murmured, coiling an arm around his neck. Linc drew away and her hand slid back down on to his chest and stilled. The realisation that he had made no move towards her all night when they were sharing the same bed suddenly clicked into place. There had been no love in the morning either, what in the past he had laughingly termed his 'speciality'. Her face clouded. So he *had* meant what he had said about not making love!

'We decided on celibacy, remember?' he drawled, promptly confirming her bleak realisation. 'It makes sense to keep things cool. Everything is . . . undecided right now.'

His reluctance spurred her on. 'But all I'm asking for is a kiss,' she purred, opening her eyes wide.

That wasn't true and they both knew it. What she wanted was Linc in bed with her, making love rashly, violently, for hour after hour until they were both replete and exhausted. She raised herself from the pillow and as her hand curled again around his neck, the sheet fell from her.

'Jude!' He pressed her back on to the softness of the water-bed, his mouth burning down on hers, his hands encircling her naked breasts, his fingers fondling the silky tips. She whimpered, arching her back and rubbing herself against the hard male thrust of his body. As he buried his face in the ashen curtain of her hair, kissing her, murmuring words of love, she grew mad with happiness. His lips were parted as he etched a path across her jaw down to her throat, nibbling and tasting the warm sleepy skin with the pointed rapier of his tongue. 'Jude, my Jude,' he muttered as his dark head bent to her breast, moistening the rigid nubs until she whimpered again. Almost without knowing it, she began to drag at his shirt, at his belt, yearning for the naked feel of him against her.

'Stop!' he protested, raising his head and frowning at her as though he wasn't sure who he was telling to stop, her or himself.

'Linc, love me, please. Linc, darling!' she implored, her fingers tearing at the cotton knit shirt, dragging it high across his chest where the dark sheen of his skin was thick with hairs. She smoothed her fingers across the hard expanse and when she felt his muscles clench she realised he was aroused almost to the point of no return.

'Stop!' he said again, wrenching himself from her, his chest rising and falling with the harsh rasp of his breathing. He swept to his feet, towering above her. 'Quit giving me a hard time,' he snarled.

Judith stared at him. 'A hard time?' she echoed.

'I feel as though I'm running a three-ring circus. 'There's Magda perpetually acting the spoilt child, Kee-Ann who has been dependent on me for the past year and who's still a worry, and now you!' He drew a hand wearily across his brow. 'I don't know what you want of me, Jude. One minute you're determined we mustn't make love and the next you're enticing me into bed.'

His rejection cut deep. 'You were willing,' she responded, yanking the sheet back up to her chin, disturbed by the mention of Kee-Ann.

'I'm a red-blooded male and naturally I was willing, but it doesn't make sense, does it? Not if you don't want a child. I've told you where I stand on that.' His jaw tightened. 'Hell! nothing makes sense any more. I need time to work things out.'

'Take your time,' she said airily, sitting up in bed and holding the sheet to her breasts. 'Take all the time you need.'

Adrenalin was surging in her veins. She knew why he needed time, why Kee-Ann was worrying him. He must be well aware of the danger of pregnancy and he was waiting to see what happened. Now she realised that by refusing to sleep with her he was determinedly pushing a wedge between them. Perhaps in planning to leave Penang he was preparing a way of escape if life became too hot to handle? Her heartbeat quickened as she thought back to Kee-Ann's revelation. It was true there had been no mention of love or a role for Linc in her future, but she was a calculating young woman. Suppose she *did* want him and was involved in some kind of devious game? Mr Cheng had stressed it was Kee-Ann's determination which had resulted in her travelling north into Thailand with Linc. She had arranged to get what she wanted on that occasion, might she not be arranging to get what she wanted now?

'Is Kee-Ann in love with you?' Judith blurted out before she could stop herself, her thoughts taking substance and surprising her.

She noticed the question didn't surprise Linc, although he did consider his reply for a moment, subjecting her to a probing look. 'Why do you ask that?'

Now she was lost for words, unable to explain. 'It . . . er . . . it strikes me she's . . . well . . . er . . . secretive.'

He brushed his beard with the back of his hand. 'I agree, but I can assure you love doesn't come into it, at least not love as we know it.'

Frowning, she was about to ask him to explain when there was a rapid knocking on the bedroom door.

'Wayne's on the telephone, and he wants to speak to you, Lincoln,' Magda yelled.

'What a thrill!' came the dry retort.

Judith bit into her toast. Life was a charade, she decided gloomily as she listened to the conversation at the breakfast table. Magda wasn't the only one who should have been on the stage, for she and Linc were actors, too, repeating their lines with stiff attention to the etiquette of life. They were acting out roles, and each sentence they exchanged appeared to be soaked in an undercurrent of suspicion and doubt. She could have accepted a degree of artificiality in the first hours of their reunion after a year apart, but not this—this contrived pretence that everything was fine when it most certainly was not!

Linc's displeasure had spilled over on to Wayne again, unfairly she thought. He had been brief almost to the point of rudeness on the telephone, merely saying he did not intend to discuss business right now but would do so later in the day when they visited. That would be another sham. Everyone would go through the motions of seeming delighted to be in each other's company when, in truth, they were all too involved with their own private obsessions to care genuinely one way or the other.

'Cy's a real gem about the house,' Magda trilled. 'I was worried about the roof, Lincoln. You remember you took a look at it eighteen months back?'

He gave a vague nod.

'I know you said it was fine,' she continued, 'but I couldn't settle. It creaked so much at night, somebody could have been up there.' Scarlet-tipped fingers wafted. 'And me, all alone in the house.'

'Why would anyone climb on to the roof in the middle of the night?' he asked reasonably as he reached for the marmalade. 'In any case you have a bedside phone, why didn't you call the cops?'

Coy lashes fluttered. 'I did, on several occasions. The officers are so charming. But the last time when I phoned the lieutenant who came round explained that they are very overworked and that I shouldn't contact them unless I actually catch a sight of an intruder.' She dabbed at the corners of her mouth with a napkin. 'He was an intellectual.'

'Who was?' Linc mumbled.

'Why, the lieutenant! Didn't I tell you about the wonderful discussion we had about Shakespeare?'

He raised incredulous brows.

'You'll be interested in this, Judith,' Magda pronounced, not bothering to wait for a response.

As Magda proceeded with a verbatim report, Judith fidgeted. Her mother-in-law had an irritating habit of shooting anything connected with England, no matter how tenuously, into her court on the blind assumption it would be of nailbiting interest, but it never was.

'And how does this tie in with Cy?' she managed to ask as Magda stopped for breath.

Her mother-in-law looked blank for a moment and then she laughed. 'Well, you see. . . .' she began, and was off again.

Linc pushed back his chair. 'I'm driving along to the helicopter pad,' he announced.

His mother stopped mid-flow. 'Again? You've been once this morning already.'

'A chopper's coming in from the airport and I'd like to talk over a couple of matters with the pilot.'

'If you're going into work then I shall, too,' Judith declared, rising to her feet. When she saw the yellow lights in his eyes flash with anger, she tossed her head. 'I'm sure Magda won't mind if I'm away for a short while?'

'Go ahead. I'd like time to shampoo my hair and lacquer my nails.' The older woman stretched out her hands before her. 'Perhaps a softer shade would look prettier in this climate?'

Judith swung to her husband. 'Would it be too much trouble for you to drop me off at the hotel?' she asked in honeyed tones.

'You said you weren't going in today,' he accused, sticking his hands into his pockets.

'When I made that decision I wasn't aware you intended to desert me,' she rejoined, treating him to a phoney smile.

He glared at her from beneath his thick lashes. 'I'll

only be away an hour at the most, so it's not worth
your visiting the shop.'

'That's your opinion! You can collect me when
you've finished your discussion and then we'll motor on
down to see Wayne and Esther.' She tripped away
towards the bedroom.

'You deserve to be . . .' he muttered.

'Deserve to be what?' she demanded over her
shoulder.

He came in behind her and closed the door, shutting
out Magda's verbose ponderings on the most favourable
shade of nail polish. 'To be well and truly laid,' he
snapped, and his anger turned him into a stranger
again.

Her cocky defiance thudded to the ground like a lead
balloon. 'But that could result in disaster,' she said
quietly, thinking of Kee-Ann.

He scowled. 'It depends on your point of view.'

The short drive to the Sentosa Country Club was
accomplished in silence. Linc deposited her at the
entrance without comment and accelerated away. In
retaliation Judith flashed a brilliant smile at an
unsuspecting tourist who stood aside to allow her to
pass by into the hotel, and he nearly dropped his
camera in delighted confusion. Blind to his reaction, she
stomped angrily away up the staircase, leaving him
gazing after her in stunned admiration.

Exactly what did Linc expect her to do? she fumed.
Neglect Mandarin Antiques and sit around like a good
little girl twiddling her thumbs and waiting for him to
reach a decision over Kee-Ann's predicament? But the
business was her lifeline. It had been the one thing
which had kept her sane and functioning in the past and
she refused to relinquish it carelessly now. One fact was
certain, her future was insecure. Even if the possible
child was not Linc's, and that, she knew, was a fragile

hope, her life would never be the same again. Could she accept his condemnation of the shop and her success with it, and follow where he led without question? A teardrop brimmed and she wiped it hastily away, breaking her step at the record shop in order to gather some composure before she greeted Rosiah. Unseeing, she stared at the garish covers of the long-playing records. Such subservience was against her nature; a marriage where she suppressed her natural spirit would be no marriage at all. She accepted that in their first year together she had been content for Linc to be in control, but they had been in the process of working through their relationship when he had disappeared. In the interim she had changed, circumstances had nurtured her independent streak and now it could not be denied. If there was no baby and they settled down to starting their life afresh, then Linc must be made to understand that she wasn't prepared to be a part of his three-ring circus. She would make no demands on him. She wanted to live alongside him, not in his shadow, and if he wasn't prepared to accept that. . . .

The man from the record shop emerged on to the threshold to beam at her. 'Good morning, Mrs Cassidy, Mr Cheng came to see me earlier today and I mentioned you had shown an interest in taking over my lease. He was delighted.' He lowered his voice and gave a broad wink. 'If you twisted his arm I suspect you could persuade him to lower the rent. Mandarin Antiques is doing so well that it attracts many customers to the arcade and all the traders benefit.'

Judith gave a wan smile. 'Thank you, I'll bear that in mind.'

It was almost two hours later that Linc appeared.

'You've been a long time,' she accused, jamming her sunglasses on to her nose and hiding from him.

For once the antiques had bored her and she had

spent the time exploring the hidden stresses in their relationship, trying to define Linc's fluctuating moods. His desire for her was genuine enough, but wasn't that merely a physical reaction? The chemistry between them had always been explosive and even the distraction she sensed within him disappeared when he held her in his arms, but the sexual pleasure they shared was only a segment. In the past their relationship had been blessed with far more. They had been in tune in so many other ways.

Now she felt emotionally bruised and vulnerable, too vulnerable to cope successfully with any further indifference—for at last she had decided that, at heart, Linc must be indifferent. Indifferent to her, to the shop, to Wayne and to Penang, indifferent to everything which mattered to her. A stream of his attitudes had floated through her head and basically they all added up to a single conclusion—indifference. It was obvious he had something on his mind, something demanding his attention, something which absorbed him, and that could only be Kee-Ann!

'I've been up to the penthouse,' he explained, confirming her fears with such deadly accuracy that she faltered in her step beside him.

'But ... but you were there last night,' she said, resuming her pace.

He flashed her a look of impatience. 'I told you, I'm worried about Kee-Ann. She's being evasive, but I'll get the truth out of her if it kills me.'

Judith didn't know what to say to that, though she had a gruesome idea she was the one destined to be the corpse, not Linc. 'Did ... didn't you go and see the pilot?' she asked, rapidly changing the subject as they went outside into the bright sunshine.

'Yes, I did. We had a long talk which was very worthwhile.'

She breathed a sigh of relief. At least he hadn't spent

the entire two hours closeted with the Chinese girl. She climbed into the Mini beside him. 'Why won't you settle for Wayne's account of what's been happening?' she demanded, finding escape in a side issue.

Linc finished winding down his window and turned to her, taking hold of the sidepieces of her sunglasses and pushing them up on to the top of her head. She blinked.

'I like to watch those expressive blue eyes of yours,' he said gravely. 'So full of indignation when I malign your saviour.'

She lowered her lashes, uneasily aware he wasn't joking.

He rested a hairy arm across the back of her seat. 'Wayne will give me the facts as he sees them, but you know as well as I do that he'll also tell me exactly what he thinks I want to hear. As I need to know the unvarnished truth, I prefer to go elsewhere.'

'He *does* tell the unvarnished truth,' she retaliated with a spark of temper.

'Occasionally, but not one hundred per cent of the time. However, from all the reports I've received so far it appears business is booming and the company is crying out for expansion.'

'Which makes it an excellent time to walk away,' she cut in bitterly.

'I haven't reached a decision,' he stressed with scarcely concealed impatience.

'Then you made a mistake when you revealed your ideas to Magda. In less than a couple of days she'll have distributed the news to the entire population of Penang!'

He lifted the heavy hair from her neck and began to stroke the skin with cool fingers. 'Don't be testy. I agree that a premature leak would be unfortunate, so I took the precaution of swearing my mother to secrecy.'

'Ha! some secrecy.'

'Temper, temper, my blue-eyed spitfire,' he smiled. 'I admit that initially I was too hasty, but now I've had time to consider your success with the antiques and it seems to me we need to have a long discussion.' He bent to kiss the warm cord of her throat.

'When?' she demanded, sitting stiffly, not daring to react. It was a breakthrough. At last he was including her in his schemes.

'Not yet.' He kissed her neck a second time, then his lips parted and he took the flesh between his teeth, biting it softly. 'Has anyone ever told you you have the smoothest skin in the most delectable places?' he murmured.

'Yes.'

He raised his head. 'Who?'

'A man I used to know.' Her mind was spinning. Why wouldn't he discuss the future *now*? The only reason for his refusal must be Kee-Ann—her confirmed pregnancy would drastically alter the future for them all. Judith began to feel ill.

'Which man?'

'One of my many lovers,' she bit out, pulling the sunglasses back down on to her nose, hiding again. 'He was strong and sensual, and he almost ate me alive. He did the most wonderfully erotic things to me.'

Linc gave a smug smile. 'And once he took you on honeymoon to the Caribbean and made love to you morning, noon and night for fourteen days non-stop.'

'How did you guess?' Suddenly she was unable to resist the warmth in his brown eyes, with the sun lines crinkling the corners. She put her hand on his wrist. 'Take me there again, Linc. *Now*. Let's just pack our bags and go today, please.' It was a cry from the heart.

'Honey, it's a great idea, but we can't. You know we can't. Life isn't as simple as that. There are so many other things to consider.'

'Like Kee-Ann,' she said faintly.

He looked down at her fingers, pale gold against the sultry shade of his arm. 'Yes, and we have Magda staying with us, and there's Mandarin Antiques.'

'Damn Mandarin Antiques!' she cried impulsively.

He chuckled. 'Hey, calm down, the shop's a good investment, you can't just up and leave it.'

Amazement at his words stretched her eyes wide.

When he saw her surprise he gave a one-sided grin of embarrassment. 'Mr Cheng was regaling me with tales of your business acumen. I didn't realise you had such a flair.'

'Wayne told you I'd improved things since Audrey's time.'

'Exactly!'

'And *I* told you!'

He sat back and switched on the ignition. 'I mistakenly suspected that Wayne had brainwashed you into believing you had done better than you really had,' he admitted, shifting the gear lever into first.

Judith's temper revved into action. 'You really think I'm so malleable and lacking in sense that I'd go along with someone else's opinion!'

Infuriatingly he grinned. 'I did, honey, but no longer.'

'If you weren't driving this car, I'd hit you.'

'Don't try it,' he warned and there was no trace of humour.

She threw him a sidelong glance, unhappily aware that although she appeared to have won a battle, she certainly hadn't won the war.

As they walked into the bungalow Magda gabbled a quick goodbye and jammed down the telephone. 'Just speaking with Cy,' she announced, looking guilty.

'I trust you've not been chattering nonstop to the States for the past hour. Our telephone account won't stand it,' Linc warned.

'It was short and sweet,' she assured him, then she smiled and began to prance before him like a mannequin. 'How do you like my outfit?'

'Great,' he said, reliable as always, and Magda patted her hair in self-congratulation.

It had to be admitted she was an eyeful in a polka-dotted white on black trouser-suit, with a black scarf tied at her neck and jet earrings dangling. Her hair was a bouffant mass of curls, her face vividly painted. In contrast Judith felt curiously subdued in a loose carnation-pink smock with matching espadrilles, her only adornment being the simple gold studs in her ears and her wide wedding band.

Linc suggested they have lunch at Batu Ferringhi Beach on their journey south, and they ate a leisurely meal beneath an umbrella-shaded table. Only yards away, beyond the close-cropped lawn, the sea sparkled like sapphires in the sunshine, and gradually Judith began to relax.

'Do you think we could visit the Snake Temple?' Magda asked as they climbed back into the car. 'Ah Fong called in at the bungalow while you were out this morning and she told me the gods there had answered her prayers.' The plucked brows arched. 'At least I *think* that's what she meant.'

'You're right,' Judith confirmed and she couldn't help laughing. She had seen Ah Fong and Magda in conversation and was astonished that any glimmer of understanding could ever penetrate. Both women talked nonstop, never pausing to enquire if they were being understood. She was sure Magda's Californian twang was as difficult for Ah Fong to grasp as her pidgin English was for the American woman.

When they reached the Snake Temple, Linc parked among the ranks of cars and they joined other tourists who were risking death as they darted across the busy road between speeding lorries and motor bikes to reach the haven of the steps which led up to the stone-pillared entrance. At the side of the steps were gift shops and stalls selling a variety of refreshments, ranging from sugar-cane juice and coconuts to pork floss. Magda spent a long time choosing a selection of postcards to send back home and then together they all climbed the granite steps.

As they reached the scarlet doors the older woman wrinkled her nose. 'What's that smell?'

'Joss sticks,' Linc explained, jerking his head towards wooden pedestals where grey smoke was drifting from clutches of the thin sticks. Madga sniffed and turned down her mouth into disapproval. He grinned. 'Live here long enough and you get to like it, like the smog in L.A.'

Regally she ignored his jibe and turned to point at the roof of the temple. 'My word! just look at that,' she breathed in admiration.

The red tiles were decorated with sculptures of dragons and other exotic oriental beasts, all brightly painted in cobalt and crimson, gold and green. Without warning a snake appeared at the top of one of the gold-lettered pillars and slid noiselessly to the ground. It stilled for a moment, black tongue flicking out, before vanishing into a flowerpot.

Magda clutched Linc's arm and shuddered. 'Ugh! Are they poisonous?'

'There are vipers, so I guess some are, but I've never heard of anyone being bitten.'

There were more snakes, long and short, plump and pencil-thin, inside the temple writhing among the carvings of the prayer tables, or curled up on the altars and among the leaves of potted palms.

'I'm scared stiff,' Magda announced in a loud voice, drawing amused glances from the less squeamish. A photographer was doing a roaring trade taking photographs of children with snakes coiled around their necks and on their heads, and Magda shrieked in horror. Her yelps as she discovered more and more snakes echoed throughout the temple, and Judith wandered off, needing to separate herself from the noisy display. Linc was being patient and long-suffering, and she supposed he should be applauded. But why was he so tolerant of Magda's foolish attitudes and yet so unfair when it came to her own feelings? she wondered. He employed two different criteria. Where was his sense of justice? Finally they joined forces.

'Thank goodness you don't act like that,' he whispered. 'The helpless-little-woman performance leaves me cold.'

'Does it?' she retorted, but she didn't believe him. Indeed, Magda's behaviour achieved what it was designed to achieve—her son's undivided attention and everyone else's, for that matter. All his life Linc had responded to his mother's pleas for help though he was well aware most of them were fake, merely ways to grab his attention when she was going through a dull patch.

And now he was distracted by Kee-Ann's plight! Judith's stomach twisted as she silently climbed into the back seat of the car. Linc had always been open and honest with her in the past, but no longer. Why couldn't he be like Wayne? she fretted. Wayne was unfailingly kind and understanding, delighted that the shop was doing well, always ready with a word of encouragement. Okay, so perhaps he did show a slight tendency to tell you what you most wanted to hear, but that was preferable to Linc's cold scepticism. Denying both her and Wayne's reports, he had obstinately refused to believe that Mandarin Antiques was a viable proposition until Mr Cheng had convinced him.

Blasting a fanfare on the horn, Linc swung into the drive of the white-stuccoed house. 'Sounds like a toy trumpet,' he remarked, arching a brow.

Judith scowled at the back of his dark head, then

turned quickly to grin with pleasure as Wayne appeared at the front door. The comforting sight of his lanky frame prompted a rush of affection. *He* hadn't altered his appearance, he was the same constant friend. Greetings were exchanged as they all clambered out of the car, and after his aunt had leapt on Wayne with cries of joy, it was Judith's turn. Rashly she allowed her gratitude at his steady reliability to overwhelm her and she slipped her arms around his waist, hugging herself to him. 'It's lovely to see you,' she smiled, and meant it.

'If you greet him like this after less than two days apart I dread to think what it must be like after a week,' Linc remarked coldly, his eyes flicking over the pair of them with distaste. 'Where's Esther?'

His disdain triggered off a need for defiance, and, standing on tiptoe, Judith reached up and kissed Wayne's cheek.

Linc pushed his hands deep into his trouser pockets. 'If you two could bear to break up the clinch, I said where's Esther?' His voice was louder than necessary, and hard.

'Changing the baby,' Wayne told him, giving a sheepish grin as he backed out of her embrace.

Suffocating rage swelled in Judith's throat. Linc was back to his tricks, intimidating Wayne, and his cousin was too good-natured to fight for survival. It was high time Linc met his match and learned that he couldn't casually ride roughshod over everyone and certainly not over her! She tucked a possessive arm through Wayne's, leaving Linc and Magda to follow them into the house. 'Linc had intended to leave Penang,' she announced in a cool clear voice, aware that he was alert to every nuance of her conversation. 'Now he's having doubts.'

She knew she was revealing his plans at her heart's peril, but she didn't care. So what if he had decided he was now prepared to talk things over? It was still on the time scale *he* dictated, not hers. Bad luck, buster! she spat privately, you made the problem, *you* cope with it!

'Leaving?' Wayne echoed in dismay.

'Doubts?' Magda gasped simultaneously.

As the four of them stood in the centre of the room the frosty glare of Linc's eyes struck a chill inside her and the adrenalin rush of defiance faltered.

'Do you want to leave?' Wayne demanded, looking down at her.

'Education is better for children in the States,' Magda babbled.

Judith flounced from Linc's gaze to confront her mother-in-law. 'That's totally irrelevant. We don't have any children.'

'Nor seem likely to,' he drawled, deserting the group and making for the staircase. 'Is Esther upstairs?'

Distractedly Wayne nodded. 'In the nursery, first left.' He turned back to Judith as Linc pounded up the stairs, two at a time. 'He can't abandon the company,' he said, his voice rising to a plea.

'He's already been out of it for a year.' Wearily she wished she could retract her statement. What inner demon had prompted her to announce Linc's half-formed plans and cause chaos? He'd sworn Magda to silence and admitted that there was more to the future than just his wishes, so what was the reason for her wretched moment of perversity? She didn't know.

With a smile Magda settled herself down in a chair and took out her compact. 'His doubts can't be serious,' she decided smugly, puckering her lipsticked mouth in the mirror. 'I'm sure he will decide to settle in San Francisco. It will be marvellous, he'll be able to visit me every week. It's only a short hop by air.'

'And are you going too, Judith?' Wayne asked, perplexed. 'What will happen to Mandarin Antiques? Do you intend to open another store in the States?'

'Judith isn't prepared to leave Penang yet,' Magda said vaguely, filling the gap when Judith struggled to find something to say.

Wayne frowned. 'I don't understand. . . .'

'Don't try,' Linc ordered, coming down the staircase with Robbie in his arms. Esther hurried close behind him and a proud smile travelled across her face as Magda gave a little cry of delight and swept over to pounce on the baby with lavish declarations of pleasure.

Judith's heart turned itself inside out. The baby was holding on to one of Linc's tanned fingers and trying to shove it into his mouth. Linc was laughing. Tears pricked behind her eyes. This could have been her baby—hers and Linc's. Through a blur of distress she watched him wiggle his finger and rub his chin gently against the baby's head, making him crow with glee as the beard tickled. Unable to stand the poignancy any longer, she spun on her heel and stumbled out into the garden, blind to everyone, everything. All the pent-up loss of her own child rose in her throat and it was as much as she could do to stop herself from sobbing out loud. She rammed her knuckles against her teeth, fighting for control.

'What's the matter?' Wayne asked, coming out to join her.

She gulped, diamond-bright tears glistening on the thick lashes. 'I'm sorry, it's just that . . . that seeing Robbie makes me realise how very much I regret losing my own baby.'

'Sugar,' he said softly. His tenderness was too much to bear and Judith went into his arms, aware it was wrong, knowing unhappily it should be Linc who was holding her close and whispering words of comfort. But where was he? Carelessly playing with the baby as Magda and Esther cooed words of admiration.

It was several minutes before she regained control. 'Some ice maiden,' she said, trying to smile through her tears.

Wayne grinned encouragingly and lent her his

handkerchief. 'We'll have a walk around the garden and look at the plants while you recover.'

She smiled at him as they did a tour of inspection. He was so understanding; if only Linc. . . . But immediately they entered the lounge she felt his disapproval.

'Where have you been?' he demanded, his voice grating with reproach. 'Has my cousin been showing you his prize bougainvillea, the biggest and best in town?'

'Can I hold Robbie?' she asked, ignoring the barbed comment.

Esther smiled her proud mother's smile and handed over the baby. Swallowing down a painful lump of despair, Judith cuddled him close.

Linc watched her for a moment, his dark eyes impassive, then turned away. 'I'd like to talk business. Can we go into the study?' he said to Wayne.

The two men disappeared, and there was little necessity for Judith to join in the conversation between Esther and her mother-in-law, which was just as well, for her mind was in turmoil. As Esther regaled Magda with tales of Robbie's eating habits, Robbie's efforts to stand up, Robbie's general progress, and Magda responded with choice tidbits about Cy and police officers and this season's fashion shades of nail polish, she sat mute, holding on to the baby.

'We'll be off now,' Linc announced in a tone which brooked no argument, when he and Wayne returned to the room half an hour later. Politely he brushed aside Esther's offer of a meal, shook hands with his cousin, chucked the baby under his chin, and had Judith and Magda installed in the car before either of them could find time to protest.

'Fancy a trip up Penang Hill?' he asked his mother when they were heading north again. He powered into top gear. 'You might as well see all you can, because if we do leave it's probable you won't be coming out to South-East Asia again.'

'What ... what did you tell Wayne about the future?' Judith asked, trying to sound totally offhand but without success.

He threw a look of icy ferocity over his shoulder. 'Not much. Don't think that because you pre-empted me I'm going to rush into any decisions. I shall take my own time, lady, and don't you forget it.'

Magda looked on goggle-eyed, unable to come to terms with this new ruthless Linc. Judith said nothing. Instead she glowered at his reflection in the driving mirror and was disconcerted when he abruptly switched his eyes from the road and his gaze slammed into hers, forcing her to lower her lashes in confusion.

Linc bought tickets and they passed through the turnstile on to the crowded platform to await the funicular railway which would carry them over two thousand feet from the Lower Station up to the summit of Penang Hill. The jostling crowd of local Malays and Chinese, with a smattering of European tourists, waited impatiently, and there was one almighty scramble for seats when the train arrived. Judith found herself wedged on a slatted wooden bench between Linc and his mother.

'Gee, isn't this fantastic?' Magda breathed, as the small train began its laborious journey up through the wooded hillside, leaving the noise and humid heat far below. Judith stared out of the window at the woodland view, acutely conscious of the wide shoulder pressed against hers, the masculine thigh which grazed hers with every movement of the train.

'It'll be cooler at the top, around sixty-five degrees, which makes a delightful change for tired nerves.' Linc sounded as though he was quoting from a tourist guide. A change for tired nerves! That was exactly what she needed.

The sun was falling in the sky as they left the carriage

at the Upper Station. The crowds quickly dispersed,
everyone making for their own favourite vantage point,
for watching the sunset from Penang Hill was a popular
excursion. They wandered through the flower gardens
and then paused, marvelling at the view. A panorama
of golden-pink clouds, hazy fields, a patchwork of
coloured tiled roofs and towering skyscrapers, spread
out before them like a painter's canvas. After a minute
or two Magda grew restless, but with her usual aplomb
struck up a conversation with an elderly Indian
gentleman who was standing nearby, and tottered off
beside him on her high heels to locate a telescope.

'It's a great view, isn't it?' Judith commented as she
and Linc stood together looking out across the island.
A long silence had stretched between them, a silence she
needed to break.

'Great,' he agreed, gazing down at her. A nerve
throbbed in his temple. There seemed to be something
struggling inside him, and he gave a sigh of
exasperation. His discomposure comforted her; at least
it was preferable to his indifference. She realised now
that it had been a desire to break through his damnable
indifference which had prompted her premature
declaration of his plans.

'You sure scared the daylights out of Wayne,' he
said, and she heard a hint of laughter in his voice.
Glancing sideways she saw a grin lurking in the corner
of his mouth. 'You intended to spoil my day, honey,
but instead you ruined his!' He started to chuckle at the
irony.

Judith forced a stiff little smile and stared out at the
view. Below them lights stabbed on in the dusk-dotted
lines of street lamps, white strips in the housing blocks,
red and blue neon advertisements in George Town,
yellow beacons pin-pricking the path of ships on the
sea.

So he had unmasked her, so what! And yet his

amusement began to seep into her. Midway between laughter and pique, she risked another glance at him, and that was her undoing, for when her eyes met his he broke out into a gale of laughter, and gathered her up in his arms.

'Lord! You're a troublemaker,' he exclaimed, holding her against him so that she felt the delight at her bad behaviour rippling through his body. He kissed her ear. 'What on earth have I done to deserve you? I don't kick cats and I'm good to my mother. A year ago I had a sweet, loving, obedient wife who only stepped out of line occasionally, but now . . .' He tilted his head and swore softly. 'Now I feel as though I'm married to a totally different woman.'

'And don't you like it?' she demanded, deliberately needling him, deliberately forcing a reply.

'It's sure as hell not dull!'

'That's no answer,' she retorted as a kind of anger welled up inside her at his lack of commitment.

'I plead the Fifth Amendment. You'll have to give me time to get to grips with the idea of possessing a new wife.'

'You don't possess me, Linc,' she flared, stepping out of his arms.

'No, honey, I don't.'

His instant agreement annoyed her intensely, and having gone so far some madwoman inside her head enticed her on. Challenging blue eyes blasted gunfire. 'I don't belong to anyone.'

He folded his arms. 'As you wish.'

'It's all your fault,' she pouted, knowing she was behaving like a peevish child and yet unable to stop herself.

'What is?'

'Oh . . . everything!' she said wildly, running her hands through her hair, lifting the weight from the nape of her neck.

'Would you have been happier if I'd never come back?' he asked in a careful voice, his brown eyes fixed on her.

'I'd have been happier if you'd never disappeared in the first place,' she slashed, suddenly blaming him for his captivity. 'Then none of this would have happened.'

'None of what?' he demanded.

Her thoughts travelled to Kee-Ann ... Kee-Ann and Linc, and the possibility the girl could be pregnant. Helplessly she shrugged, remembering her promise of secrecy.

'For heaven's sake, if you're trying to tell me something, say it!' he insisted, his gaze suddenly bleak and alien. His mouth was a straight line, virtually lost in the dark growth of his beard. He's a stranger, she realised, panic-stricken, a total stranger. 'Jude, we've always been honest with each other,' he told her earnestly. 'Even if it hurts, please tell me what's bothering you. It's vital I hear it from you.'

She shook her head from side to side in rapid gestures of protest. 'I can't. I just can't.'

He frowned out at the orange ball of the sun sinking into the horizon. 'You and Kee-Ann both, she's hiding something from me too,' he muttered.

Her heart contracted at his mention of the Chinese girl.

Linc sighed, then after a moment straightened his shoulders as though reaching a decision. 'I'll allow you a week to work things out, Jude, and then you must decide what you want to do. We can't start over again unless we're honest with each other. There can't be trust without the truth, honey, even if it is painful. Okay?'

'Okay,' she agreed reluctantly. Before the week was out perhaps Kee-Ann's dilemma would be resolved, and if not she would visit the girl and insist Linc be told.

'I'll allow Kee-Ann a week's grace, too,' he said, as though he was talking to himself. 'After that I intend to force everything out into the open and make Cheng Boon Seng aware of my suspicion.'

'And what's that?' Judith asked, unable to stop herself. There was a long pause in which her heart froze as she dreaded the answer.

Linc's jaw jutted. 'That she's pregnant and it's all my fault.'

CHAPTER SEVEN

AT his harsh revelation, her lower lip had trembled. Linc *was* the father! It was only when he had finally admitted he was to blame that she realised how desperately she had been clinging to the slender hope that some other man had been responsible. But brutally he had dashed her tenuous lifebelt from her grasp, leaving her to drown in a sea of desolation. On shaking legs she had reeled from him, blind to his outstretched hand as she had rushed for the haven of the bench where Magda was chatting to the Indian gentleman.

And now, six days later, she was once again seeking solace in her business life. She couldn't decide if it was a cowardly retreat, but she knew that without the distraction of Mandarin Antiques her nerves would have been in a far worse state. After the weekend Linc had announced his decision to start flying again, and though he had spent time on Monday morning with the reporter, he had then made a rapid exit for the helicopter pad, only returning in time for the evening meal. Magda, too, was occupied; her Indian friend, Mr Jeyaretnam, had invited her to join him on a day-long coach tour of Penang. Automatically Judith had drifted back to the shop and a pattern had been set. Each following day saw Linc involved with the helicopters, his mother sightseeing, while Judith devoted herself to her antiques. Mr Cheng had called to enquire if she was interested in leasing the adjacent unit, but she had stalled. Sunday, she thought, her heart thumping unevenly, on Sunday I'll reach a decision.

Gradually as the days passed, she had forced herself to consider what the future could hold. There had been no news from Kee-Ann, so the likelihood of her being pregnant now seemed a reality. Judith knew that no matter what had happened in the jungle, she still loved Linc and always would. Fondly she recalled the rapture they had shared at the beginning of their marriage, but then a storm broke loose in her memory as she thought of the savage pain of the year apart—a year when she had lost her child and perhaps, she admitted for the first time, her husband. His physical loss had been traumatic, but even that paled beside the devastating loss of their emotional affinity, for now they were two strangers, with nothing to say to each other.

Each night he had kept his distance, briefly kissing her cheek before turning from her to fall asleep, seemingly within seconds. Judith, on the other hand, had lain awake until the early hours, despising his iron control and yet beginning to wonder if it *was* control, or merely further proof of his growing indifference. Since their conversation atop Penang Hill he had made no further mention of Kee-Ann, but she sensed his continual distraction. At times she felt his eyes upon her as though he was wondering what role she would play in his future, or, indeed, if there was any future for them both. Slowly, insidiously, the idea that he might wish to leave her and marry Kee-Ann crept into her mind. Although there was no reason to believe he loved the girl, Linc was an honourable man, a man of duty. He cared about family life; hadn't he stood by Magda all these years, coping with her foolishness when many another man would have run out of patience long ago and left her to her own devices? If there was a child it seemed probable that his commitment to the Chinese girl would be just as strong.

At six o'clock sharp Judith locked the shop door, bade farewell to Rosiah and made her way along the shopping arcade and out into the dusk. These last few hours were the calm before the storm, she realised despondently, for tomorrow she would tell Linc she was prepared to give him his freedom. In the empty night hours she had thought hard and long, and there seemed to be no alternative but for them to part. She knew Linc would never agree to Kee-Ann's arranging an abortion. It was against his principles, and maybe, deep down, that was what the girl wanted? By keeping the baby she would be tying herself to Linc for ever, and Judith knew his highly developed sense of obligation would make him accept that his place must be with the mother of his child.

Yet again Magda was chattering away on the telephone when she arrived home. Judith went into the kitchen to fetch a tumbler of iced lime and when she returned her mother-in-law replaced the receiver and giggled. 'Cy rang,' she explained breathlessly.

Raising her brows, Judith pushed her own problems aside. 'He must be keen, that's the fourth time in four days.' She dropped down on to the sofa. If only Linc was so ardent. . . .

'I had a fantastic day with Mr Jeyaretnam,' Magda exclaimed. 'We visited the Pagoda of Ten Thousand Buddhas, and what a climb! There are hundreds of steps, but the view from the top is marvellous. Mind you, after all the exercise and the disgusting smell of joss-sticks, I felt quite faint.' She fanned the air in front of her. 'And the heat! It must have been over a hundred in the shade. I enjoy the Californian sunshine, but this. . . .' She ran out of words and sank down beside Judith, pushing off her shoes. After a moment she asked hesitantly, 'Has Lincoln said anything more to you about moving back to the States? Whenever I broach the subject he shoots me down in flames. I guess his episode in captivity must have been a strain on his nerves.'

'There's not much wrong with his nerves,' Judith replied flatly. 'But no, we haven't discussed the future—

yet.' A pulse began to throb in her forehead. Tomorrow, tomorrow was D Day—D for discussion, for disaster, for destroying the rest of her life.

'I guess that means I must curb my impatience,' Magda grimaced. She began to unfasten the jade beads from around her neck, and her face brightened. 'This evening I would be delighted if you and Lincoln would be my guests at dinner. You have both been very kind coping with my unexpected arrival and I want to say thank you—this invitation is my little treat. Besides, Mr Jeyaretnam was telling me they lay on the most fantastic poolside barbecue at the Sentosa Country Club, so I've gone ahead and made a reservation for four.'

'Thanks very much,' Judith smiled, though secretly she wasn't too sure of the wisdom of Mr Jeyaretnam's being included. He seemed to be looming a little too large at present, and she wondered what the absent Cy's reaction would be if he knew. Finishing off the lime juice, she rose to her feet. 'I'll shower and shampoo my hair.'

'Good idea,' Magda agreed. 'I'll go and freshen up too.'

When Linc arrived home Judith was blow-drying her hair.

'Jeez, what a day! I'm worn out,' he complained, collapsing on the bed, hands behind his head.

'Grab yourself a reviving gin and tonic,' she said evenly, trying to ignore the vibrant male body stretched out before her. 'Your mother has invited us to dinner this evening.'

He rolled over to sit on the edge of the bed. 'We're not going,' he said firmly. 'I want to be alone with you tonight. I've sat through dinner every goddamn evening this week listening to Magda's silly conversation and, quite frankly, I can't take any more.'

Perhaps his nerves *were* strained, she realised with

dawning surprise. 'But it's her way of saying thank you to us,' she explained.

'Don't be naïve. Ten to one it'll be me who ends up paying, or that Indian guy. I expect he's invited too?'

'Yes, yes he is.'

He scowled. 'I'm not in the mood for making small talk with strangers. What Magda gets up to is her own concern, but count me out.' He rose to his feet and came behind her, slipping his arms around her waist, pulling her back against him. In the filmy negligee she could feel the hard imprint of his body, his sexual arousal explicit in the muscular line of his thighs. 'Tonight is the time for us to talk, honey,' he murmured into her neck. 'I can't wait any longer.'

Judith held herself tense, ignoring the double entendre. 'You said tomorrow,' she protested, now desperate for a few last hours of . . . of what, of peace, of freedom? Some freedom, when she was obsessed with the inevitability of losing him.

A large hand slid into the fold of her negligee and as his fingers reached for her breast she closed her eyes. Oh Lord! just his touch was capable of arousing her beyond belief. Beneath his hand her breast was swelling, its point tightening with incredible need. He rubbed a thumb across the dark aureole and she was forced to bite her lip to stifle a plea for his love. Drenching desire oozed from her, and it was as though she was riding a merry-go-round, her heart rising and falling in time to loud music. Linc nuzzled into the warm hollow of her throat, and there came the tantalising tickle of his beard against her skin.

'Tonight,' he said in a low voice. 'It must be tonight.'

She twisted from him. How could she make love with him if he wanted his freedom, and yet how could she resist him? If he had made another move towards her she would have surrendered without hesitation, but he held himself still. There was a ringing silence as he studied her. Surely he could read the love in her eyes? In the past they had been so much in tune, each always knowing what the other was thinking. Love me, Linc, she implored silently, but instead he sighed and turned away into the bathroom.

As she heard the rush of the shower, she sank down on to the dressing-stool. Why shy away from cold hard facts? She and Linc would never be the same again. Defiantly she resolved to meet the crisis head-on. Her blue eyes glittered as she surveyed her reflection. There was only one way to make an exit and that was in a blaze of glory. Kee-Ann might resemble a porcelain doll with her oriental charms, but Judith was confident of her own Western appeal. If Linc was destined to say goodbye, then he would know he was saying goodbye to a beautiful and desirable woman. Tossing back the fall of gleaming hair, she reached for her tray of cosmetics.

She made up her face with extra-special care. Her peach-smooth complexion needed no foundation or powder, but she applied a hint of blusher to emphasize her high cheekbones, and then concentrated on her eyes. She used a blend of shadows—dove-grey and silver with a feathery line of kohl, then several coats of sooty mascara to thicken her lashes. Finally she coloured in her lips with a pearly shade of rose-geranium.

Searching through the rail of dresses, her hand picked out a silver sheath dress. It was well over a year since she had dared to wear it, for Linc had called it her 'follow me' dress when he was being polite and something far more graphic when he wasn't. It was a spectacularly seductive creation, the back of the dress being non-existent, and the strapless bodice held in place only by silver laces which criss-crossed the length of her spine. The skirt clung tight, a split to thigh level allowing her room to walk. It was an outfit which needed to be worn with an air of reckless bravado, and this evening it suited her mood exactly.

'Wow!' he exclaimed, walking back into the room. 'I had presumed that as we're not joining Magda we'd eat at home, but since you're already dressed up I suppose the least I can do is take you out.' He reached for a dark grey silk shirt. 'But we'll come back early.'

Not if I can help it, she decided, and the sexy minx in the mirror arched a brow. Tonight she would insist on being dined and wined in style, then they would go on to one of the 'in' videotheques and dance until dawn. Tonight audacity ran in her veins and she was determined to flaunt herself before him to make him realise just what it was he was giving up.

Linc tucked his shirt into pale grey slacks.

'Thanks for the invitation, Mother,' he said as they joined Magda in the living-room. 'But Jude and I won't be coming with you this evening. We have things to discuss.'

Her face fell. 'But you *have* to come!'

'Sorry, tomorrow perhaps, but not this evening.' His deep voice was definite. 'I understand that Indian guy will be present, so I'm sure it's not too much of a disappointment if we back out. Keep tomorrow free, then we'll fix something for just the three of us.'

Magda twitched her shoulders in annoyance. 'But I want you both to come this evening,' she insisted stubbornly. Her chagrin appeared to be genuine, which was surprising, for Judith had fully expected her mother-in-law to flippantly discard the idea, being happy to dine alone with her Indian gentleman.

'I'm sorry, but no,' Linc repeated. 'Look, we'll run you down to the hotel and I'll have a word with this Mr Jeyaretnam and explain why we can't make it. Jude and I have hardly had any time alone together since I arrived home a week ago. Surely you can understand why we must refuse?'

Magda eyed him cautiously. 'You promise you'll both come and meet Mr Jeyaretnam at the poolside?'

'Yes, we will,' he agreed patiently.

'You'll come right to the poolside and speak to him, at eight o'clock?'

'Yes, if that's what'll make you happy.'

She giggled. 'Okay then, that's fine, but it must be at eight.'

Now she was content and went through the usual performance of asking Linc if he liked her outfit, twirling before him like a ballerina on a musical box. He complied with standard affability, saying all the words she wanted to hear. In her full-skirted dress of coral satin, the bodice thickly encrusted with diamanté drops and emerald sequins, Magda made her usual vivid impact on the eye, and once Linc's praise had been duly administered she chattered, without pause, all the way to the hotel.

On their arrival, Linc slipped the car keys into his pocket and took both women by the elbow, steering them through the lobby and out to the grounds at the rear of the hotel where an Olympic-sized swimming pool was set amidst tropical palms. A crescent moon and an array of stars were pasted in the night sky as neatly as if an eager child had cut them from silver paper, and fairy lights shone red, blue, yellow and green, strung from poles around the water's edge. Judith was surprised to see that the wrought-iron tables to one side of the pool were crowded with people; she hadn't realised the barbecue was so popular. As they rounded a raised bed of rampaging bougainvillea at one corner of the pool, a loud cheer rang out. Instantaneously there was the rasp of matches being struck, and candles in the centre of each of the round tables sprang into flame. A spotlight flashed on, and to her utter amazement she realised everyone was smiling and waving in their direction. A second spotlight revealed a

banner billowing—'Welcome Home Linc and Kee-Ann'
it read.

'My word!' Linc's fingers tightened on her elbow as
three rousing cheers broke out. For a moment he
seemed about to turn and make a dash for the exit, but
then he shook his head in bewilderment, accepting
defeat. 'Did you know anything about this?' he asked,
sotto voce. Stunned, she shook her head.

'It was my idea,' Magda announced proudly. 'Mrs
Cheng and I have been planning it all week. Look, the
Chengs are over there.'

Judith gazed around, returning the smiles on
friendly faces. She recognised the staff from the
helicopter company, Mr and Mrs Lim, some sailing
cronies, Ah Fong and her husband with Mimi,
Rosiah, and a wide assortment of local and European
friends. Magda bustled away to join Mr Jeyaretnam,
and, recovering his poise, Linc pulled Judith with him
to greet everyone and a crowd milled around, shaking
hands, kissing, patting Linc on the back, talking
nineteen to the dozen.

'Why didn't you give me a hint this party was being
planned?' Judith whispered to Wayne as they passed his
table. 'I might have arrived here in a tee shirt and old
shorts.'

He grinned. 'But you didn't, sugar, you look
gorgeous.'

'She always does.' Linc's voice rasped from somewhere behind.

At last they extricated themselves from the mêlée and
found themselves with Magda and Mr Jeyaretnam, and
two of the pilots and their wives. With relief they sank
down on to the vacant chairs provided.

'You must change tables with each different course,'
Magda instructed importantly. 'That way everyone gets
to hear about your experiences with those dreadful
Communists.'

Linc's brow arched. 'Thank goodness we're not having a Chinese meal with ten courses! I'd go mad if I had to repeat the same tale ten times over. Can't we just tell everyone to buy the paper tomorrow? The interview appears then. It would certainly save my vocal cords.'

'Everyone wants to hear your news first-hand,' his mother protested, not quite sure whether or not he was joking.

Pulling down his mouth into a gesture of resignation, he turned to devote his attention to the wife of one of the pilots, who was bursting with questions.

It would have been difficult not to respond to the air of happiness and general affection, and as her tension slid from her, Judith began to enjoy herself. Looking around she realised that the tables on the far side of the pool were indeed occupied by bona fide guests of the hotel, but their area had been roped off to keep the party private. Mr Cheng had spared no expense; a battery of waiters provided aperitifs and each course heralded a different choice of wine. The food was excellent—an avocado starter, charcoal-grilled steak and salad, followed by rum babas and cream, and finally a vast selection of cheeses. A stage had been erected at the outer rim of the paved area, adjoining the lawns, and members of a pop group were gradually taking their places upon it.

Once he had recovered from his initial reluctance, Linc fell in with Magda's instructions, shepherding Judith to different tables and calmly answering identical questions time and time again. She was grateful that the table where Kee-Ann and the rest of her family sat was one they didn't have time to visit.

'Thank heavens my recital's nearly over,' Linc whispered as they reached the coffee stage, and made a final move to join Wayne, Mr and Mrs Lim and some sailing friends. After coping with the inevitable flurry of questions, he lit a cigar and leant back in his chair.

'That's it,' he said firmly. 'Now, no more talk about me.'

'We'll talk about your wife,' Mr Lim grinned, with a wink at Judith. He tapped the side of his nose. 'She's a shrewd young woman, with a flair for antiques.'

Resting his arm along the back of her chair, Linc smiled. 'I'm beginning to realise that. I'm very proud of her.'

Whether it was the effect of the wine she had drunk, or the general feeling of bonhomie, Judith didn't know, but she was too mellow to point out that his pride had had to be drummed into him. Quietly she sipped her apricot brandy and decided that if this was to be their last evening together before the guillotine sliced down, it certainly couldn't be bettered.

His hand had moved from the back of her chair to her shoulder, and after casually fondling the smooth skin for a few minutes it slipped even further to below her arm, where his fingers trickled beneath the edge of her bodice to caress the side of her breast. She tried to deny the quick onrush of excitement, but failed miserably. If this was seduction then she was already in his power, unreservedly so. She gave him a sideways glance. Linc was relaxed and uncaring, as though he had no connection with the long fingers which were so expertly arousing her, sending her temperature soaring to danger level. He was sprawled in his chair, legs stretched wide, his cigar between the fingers of his free hand, the fragrant smoke drifting as he emphasised some point to a friend across the table. Oh Lord! she thought desperately, I love him so much. With a start she realised that Wayne, seated on her other side, was eyeing Linc's philandering caress, and guiltily she sat upright. His hand dropped away.

'Where's Esther?' she demanded, snapping back to life. She heard Linc move in his chair beside her, but refused to look in his direction.

'Robbie has a cold, so she didn't want to leave him,' Wayne replied.

'Oh.'

There was an unexpected roll on the drums and every head swivelled towards the stage as Mr Cheng walked up and lifted the microphone. In flowery phrases he began to express his gratitude to Linc for safeguarding Kee-Ann over the past year.

'For Pete's sake!' Linc muttered uncomfortably, inspecting the tip of his cigar with exaggerated interest as Mr Cheng waxed long and lyrical.

'A man of courage, tenacity and total integrity,' he extolled.

Judith swallowed the rest of her apricot brandy in one gulp and held out her glass for more as a waiter silently appeared. The irony was humiliating. What would Mr Cheng think when Linc was forced to reveal the true happenings of that year in captivity? She swirled the syrupy liquid around in her glass and took a swift gulp, and another. As finally their host ran out of praise, there was a round of applause and several cheers in Linc's direction.

'And now I feel it would be fitting for Linc and Kee-Ann to take the floor for the first dance,' Mr Cheng said, with a wide smile.

Linc muttered an indistinct oath before pushing back his chair and courteously walking across to Kee-Ann's table.

'I get the impression your husband's not hooked on being the centre of attention,' Wayne chuckled into her ear.

She forced a smile, watching as he led Kee-Ann out on to the paved area before the stage. How petite she was! Judith thought all over again. The pop group had struck up a love song, and the Chinese girl glided into Linc's embrace, her raven-black head barely reaching the middle of his chest. When she said something he bent to catch her words, the gesture painfully intimate, his dark head close to hers, his expression serious as he listened to what she had to say. Other couples were rising to dance.

'Shall we?' Wayne asked.

With a little toss of her head, Judith stood up. 'Why not?' she said gaily, walking ahead of him through the tables.

Wayne's arms were comforting, just what she needed after six days of rejection. He had no inhibitions about holding her close, and she nestled against him like a child seeking security from a beloved teddy bear. Although every night Linc had lain beside her, he had barely touched her, making a point of holding himself physically aloof. The rejection had cut deep, wounding her pride and her belief in herself as a loving and lovable woman. But now Wayne's fond embrace told her that *he* cared, that he would never throw her love back in her face.

As she glanced over his shoulder her heart missed a beat. Linc had taken Kee-Ann by the hand and was leading her off the dance floor into the shadows. Judith stumbled. 'Sorry,' she said, her eyes stinging with tears. 'I'm out of practice.'

'What's the matter, sugar?' Wayne asked, looking down at her. 'And don't dare to say nothing, I know you too well for that.'

Linc and Kee-Ann had vanished. She took a shuddering breath, not knowing where to start.

'It's Linc, isn't it? The bastard's not making you happy,' Wayne growled. He scanned the dancing crowd and as he realised his cousin was no longer with the party his lips tightened.

'I think it's a case of us not making each other happy, it's a two-way thing,' she pointed out.

He shook his head savagely. 'No, it's *his* fault. He used to be so committed, but now he doesn't seem to know what he wants, and this crazy scheme of pulling out of Penang. . . .' He flicked a hand at the incredulity of the idea.

'It's not crazy,' she protested, not knowing why she felt the sudden need to leap to Linc's defence. 'It does make sense. If he intends to make a break, now is the time to do it.' Resolutely she blocked out the admission that it was likely he would be leaving without her, that it would be Kee-Ann who joined him in his new life.

Wayne frowned, considering her words, and for a few minutes they danced in silence. The rhythm of the music was beginning to soothe her when, without warning, he started up again. '*You've* always enjoyed living in the tropics.'

'Yes,' she said impatiently, wishing he would let the matter rest. Linc and Kee-Ann were still missing, and when she lifted her eyes skywards she saw lights shining on high in the penthouse windows.

'*You* don't want to leave,' Wayne insisted with dogged determination.

The melody came to an end, and there was a moment or two of silence before the pop group started into the latest reggae hit. Conversation beneath the amplified blare of the guitar and drums was impossible, and Judith spread her hands wide, indicating, with relief, that now was not the time to talk. As the rhythm throbbed she and Wayne started to dance again. The raunchy beat pulled all the young people on to the floor, and within seconds it was alive with couples bobbing and weaving. She abandoned herself to the music, hips swaying seductively beneath the tight skirt of her silver sheath dress as she gyrated before her partner. The music pulsated and she flashed her wide blue eyes, smug in the knowledge that she was an appealing young woman and here was a man who desired her.

Wayne laughed delightedly, falling in with her mood. 'Sugar, you and I could really light up the town tonight,' he whispered into her ear.

Flirtatiously she smiled deep into his eyes, playing the coquette. 'Yes, we could, couldn't we?' she agreed, before pushing herself free and swaying again, enticing him with the mobile grace of her slender body.

They returned to their table when the music ended. Flushed and panting, she sank down on to a chair, and when a waiter appeared with fresh supplies of white wine she promptly drank half a glassful. She chattered gaily to Wayne and other friends at their table, but despite the lighthearted banter she was all too aware that there was still no sign of her husband and Kee-Ann. Her eyes scoured the tables. Mr Cheng was absent too; perhaps he had watched his daughter's departure and felt impelled to discover what was happening? To hell with Linc and all the problems he had caused, she thought mutinously, and she held up her empty glass, smiling as Wayne filled it to the brim.

One of the helicopter pilots asked her for the next dance and then a man from the sailing club came over. Defiantly she flirted with each, and was rewarded with a gratifying dose of male admiration. How easy men were to handle, she thought, unhappily aware that Linc was the one exception to the rule.

'My turn,' Wayne smiled when the tempo slowed to a smoochy love song, and with another swift drink of wine Judith walked back on to the dance floor and into his arms.

'I do like you,' she purred, resting against his shoulder, lightheaded with the ebb and flow of the music.

'Okay, cousin, move over,' a voice snapped, and a band of steel fingers encircled her wrist. Linc had pushed his way through the throng and was standing beside them, his stance aggressive.

Judith giggled. 'You'll have to wait,' she informed him with a wide smile of tipsy defiance.

'Like hell.' He jerked his head, crudely ordering

Wayne to leave, and obediently his cousin backed away, disappearing into the crowd. 'Didn't take him long to slink away on his white charger, did it?' Linc commented with annoying smugness, taking her firmly into his arms.

The exhilaration of the wine faded a little. 'There was no need to be so bad-mannered,'she pouted, irritated by the subservient manner in which Wayne had retreated. Why must he always comply with Linc's wishes? For a moment she was tempted to try and wriggle away, but Linc was holding her tight, his fingers splayed across the bare skin of her backbone, and she realised he would never allow her to escape.

As they moved with the music his fingers began to travel up and down her spine, scorching her skin, making her feel hot and cold, and unhappily aware of her vulnerability. The carefree haze instilled by the alcohol began to disappear. He was making love to her as they danced, his breath hot on her brow, the pressure of his long fingers increasing with relentless intensity. In protest she raised her eyes to his, but the raw desire she saw there echoed too strongly the traitorous throb of her own body. It seemed that her gaze was chained to his, she was falling headlong into those deep brown eyes disturbingly flecked with gold. The large hand against her shoulder-blades pulled her closer as the other slithered down to her hips. She was grateful that in the crush of dancers his movement went unnoticed, for he was blatantly making her aware of his arousal as he spread his legs and swayed against her.

'Linc,' she pleaded, but he took no notice. Oh Lord! to her fury she felt her nipples begin to tighten, and her dress was so fine and she was pressed against his chest.

As though reading her thoughts, he glanced down, his brow arching in arrogant male satisfaction. 'Willing participant?' he murmured.

'I . . . I don't want to dance.' If she didn't get away

from the muscular body rubbing against hers, she knew she would be unable to offer any resistance at all, and resistance was vital if they were to make a clean break. It would be foolish to allow physical desires to cloud the issue.

'Okay, we'll go sailing.' He interlaced his fingers with hers and steered her away from the dance floor to a deserted strip of shadowy lawn behind the stage.

'Sailing?' she repeated stupidly.

'Stay here, I'll not be a minute,' he ordered, striding away.

Dumbstruck, she gazed around her. Beyond the gardens, in the distance, was the jetty, boats bobbing gently alongside, riding a sea of black ink. In the silvery light of the moon she could pick out the soft surge of water as waves rolled shorewards. Linc was crazy, it was much too dark and too late to go sailing—even if she wanted to, which she didn't. It wasn't safe to be alone with him. In her present vulnerable state it was far better she keep well away. She turned back towards the dance floor. Beyond the dancing couples there was a glimpse of Wayne's fair head; he was sitting at a table, talking to someone's wife. Typical, she thought, Wayne makes a career out of chatting up other men's wives. Immediately she retracted the unkind idea, for hadn't he a heart of gold? Wasn't he genial and understanding, and wouldn't she be far safer at his side than at Linc's? Biting her lip, she took a step forward.

A hand caught her in her stride. Linc had returned and it was too late for retreat.

'Come on.' He took her hand and pulled her with him across the lawn. As she skittered after him she noticed a bottle of champagne in his free hand. 'We have to celebrate,' he smiled, noticing her look. His strides increased and Judith was forced to run, her heels click-clacking on the jetty as he made for his destination. When they reached the end of the walkway he stopped and, releasing her hand, reached into his trouser pocket for a bunch of keys.

'Mr Cheng has given us the use of his cabin cruiser,' he explained. 'And he provided the Moët et Chandon. There are paper cups on board, and towels, if we want to swim. We're free to go anywhere.'

Defiantly she spread her hands on her hips. 'Not me. I'm not going with you.'

He set the champagne on the wooden jetty and went down a shallow flight of steps to a small cabin cruiser. Calmly he began to dismantle the black canvas roof cover.

In the ensuing silence Judith heard the slap of the waves against the hull. 'I'm not going,' she repeated.

'Yes, you are.' He folded the cover, tossing it onto a bench seat behind the cockpit. 'This is an ideal opportunity. We need to be alone and to talk.' He glanced up at her and when he read the hesitation on her face, he prompted, 'Don't we?'

'Yes,' she admitted.

'Then come down here and join me, and bring the champagne.'

Reluctantly she picked up the bottle and made her way down. Linc stretched out his arms to clasp her around the waist, and lifted her easily into the boat beside him. Bending his head, he brushed his mouth against hers, and then his tongue slid out and gently caressed her lower lip. It was their secret invitation to make love.

Ignoring his sensual message, she pushed herself free of his arms. 'What ... what are we celebrating?' she asked shakily.

A muscle clenched in his jaw as he released her, but then he smiled. 'The fact that Miss Cheng is not pregnant!' He climbed fore and aft, untying the ropes and retrieving the fenders. 'It seems an excellent cause for celebration to me,' he said as he returned to the cockpit.

'It would,' she muttered unhappily, finding his glee too hard to handle.

'But don't you see, her life won't be disrupted.'

She shrugged. 'So she's been reprieved and so have you.'

'It's a helluva relief, and Cheng Boon Seng was real understanding, thank God.' He gunned the engine and the cruiser moved slowly out through the shallows towards the deeper water.

'How very convenient!'

He swung the steering wheel in an arc to follow the line of the coast. 'You should be pleased,' he retorted, frowning at her.

'Should I? Why? Naturally I'm relieved that Kee-Ann has been saved the trauma of an abortion, but it doesn't alter the fact that she *could* have been pregnant.'

'No, I agree,' he said flatly. 'Still, I'm grateful her father understood.'

'Bully for him,' she replied and discovered she was yelling, the blood exploding in her head. 'Is that all you care about? You're happy because he was magnanimous enough not to condemn you? Big deal! And I suppose now you expect me to follow suit?' She gripped the rail, steadying herself as the boat surged forward. 'Believe me, I understand too, but somehow that makes it all the harder. Do you honestly expect us to begin again now as though nothing has happened?' Abruptly her voice faded, and she bent her head, the long ashen hair obscuring her face. 'I'm sorry, but I can't. I can't pretend that knowing the child might have been ... Eurasian, doesn't matter. It's not that simple.'

Linc rubbed at the edge of his jaw. 'But it wouldn't have been Eurasian. I don't know what a mixture of Thai and Chinese is called, but it's certainly not Eurasian.'

Her blue eyes swung to his. 'Thai?'

'Sumphote was Thai.'

Hope struggled weakly within her. 'But you said *you* were responsible.'

'I wasn't the father!' he declared, staring down at her in amazement. 'Oh, heavens, honey, you never thought that. . . .' Abruptly he switched off the engine and pulled her into his arms. 'Jude, Jude, it wasn't my child. I love you too much. I'd never be unfaithful.'

'But you said it was your fault,' she whispered.

'It was my fault in as much as I encouraged the friendship between Kee-Ann and Sumphote. I felt it would make life easier and lift the tension for all of us. I was enthusiastic when he brought her books and took an interest in her.' He shook his head in disbelief. 'I was so naïve, I imagined their companionship was straight-forward, and when I realised it wasn't, I blamed myself. It had never crossed my mind that Kee-Ann might try to seduce him.'

'She seduced him?' Judith repeated faintly, her eyes wide.

He gave a bark of grim laughter. 'She might look as though butter wouldn't melt in her mouth but, believe me, when that young madam decides she wants something she goes all out to get it, no holds barred. When she first joined me in the car on our fateful journey into Thailand, she made it painfully obvious she expected to get laid and that I had been chosen as the lucky man! I had to be downright objectionable and read the Riot Act before she would understand that no way do I mess around.' He sighed. 'Now I wonder if she slept with Sumphote in retaliation or whether she's some kind of nymphomaniac!'

'And what does Mr Cheng think of all this?' she asked in a small wondering voice.

'The old guy's very pragmatic. He realises Kee-Ann comes on too strong. I told him how unhappy I felt about the whole sorry mess, but when I apologised he said it was not my responsibility. He made Kee-Ann confess her side of the tale and then I didn't feel so guilty. It appears Sumphote wasn't keen to become involved with her either, but she wouldn't take no for an answer. Over the months she wore away his resistance, but only managed to coax him into bed a couple of times. It turned out she'd been sleeping around in the States and when she came back East on holiday and family confines snapped down, she began to feel rather frustrated.' There was the crook of wryness in his smile. 'I know exactly how she felt. Which brings me to something else you and I need to discuss!'

Happiness was swelling inside her. So Linc *had* been faithful! Suddenly she was delirious, she wanted to laugh and cry, turn cartwheels over the moon and sing triumphant choruses. Instead she clung to him weakly as her delight washed over her. 'What?' Judith asked.

He wrinkled his nose. 'Celibacy—it stinks!' She giggled as his arms tightened around her and he kissed the tip of her nose. 'Okay, so you don't want us to start a family just yet, I respect that, but from now on we'll take precautions.' He shook his head from side to side in silent protest. 'There's no way I can lie in the same bed and not make love to you.' Restless hands moved along her spine to the long slow curve of her hips. 'I seem to have spent every minute of every night this past week watching you in the dark, wanting to kiss the smooth skin on your shoulders or the angle of your waist. How in hell's name I ever came up with the crazy idea I could live with you and not lay you, I'll never know! I guess I was just so damned angry when you told me to keep away that I decided to punish us both.'

Judith laughed, and, loving him, she curled her arms around his broad shoulders and drew his head down to hers. Slowly she parted her lips on his and ran the tip of her tongue across the soft fullness of his lower lip.

'Honey!' he moaned, before opening his mouth wide

on hers, forcing back her head as he kissed her hard and long. The kiss went on and on, and she reeled beneath his ardour. The devastation he wrought was complete. Giddily she clung to him as he stroked her hair and kissed her, each kiss becoming deeper and more demanding. He nuzzled a path across her cheekbone to a blue vein throbbing erratically in her neck.

'I thought we were here to talk,' she murmured as his fingers stroked the upper swell of her breast.

Passion made his smile misty. 'Nope! There's only one thing I want to do right now and that takes no talking at all.'

With gentle hands, she pushed him from her. 'There's something else you'll have to do, Linc, unless you want us to be shipwrecked.'

Snapping up his head he gazed around and then sprang into action, slamming the boat into gear, his foot hard on the throttle. They had drifted into the shallows; a few yards more and they would have beached. Now he laughed and sent the cruiser powering out into deeper water, the night breeze ruffling his hair, lifting it from his brow. 'Find us some cups, Jude, and I'll open the champagne.'

There was a stack of white paper cups on a shelf in the tiny cabin, and she brought them up to him in the cockpit where he was struggling with the cork.

'I'll steer,' she offered.

'Thanks, now I can use two hands.' There was a loud pop as the cork shot up into the air and plopped into the sea; champagne foamed riotously, spattering on to the deck and Linc's shirt. Grinning, he poured two cups. 'To us,' he smiled, raising his eyes to hers.

'To us,' she repeated, sharing his look of love.

He took over the wheel, slipping his arm around her waist, pulling her against his chest.

'You're all wet and sticky,' she protested, dubiously

eyeing the dark stains. 'Your shirt's soaked, why don't you take it off?'

His brow arched. 'You undress me. I seem to remember you're much better at it than I am.'

The adrenalin of desire began to flow in her veins, intermingling with the champagne to produce a carefree certainty that the one reason for her existence on earth was to love the tall lean-hipped man beside her. Tip of her tongue protruding gravely from between her teeth, she applied herself to the task in hand, slowly unfastening the buttons one by one, and kissing his chest as each sprang free. When the silk shirt hung loose she spread her fingers and, palms down, ran her hands across the springy cover of dark hair. 'You're beautiful,' she told him, rubbing her cheek against the thick curls, wallowing in the intoxicating feel and fragrance of him.

'Guys aren't beautiful,' he grinned, taking one hand from the steering wheel and moving her in front of him to stand in the cage of his arms as he steered.

'You are beautiful,' she insisted.

'Even with my beard?' he asked, watching her with eyes gentle with love.

'Even with your beard,' she conceded.

Dragging the shirt from his shoulders, she pulled it free and tossed it towards the bench seats in the rear of the boat. The breeze billowed. 'Oh dear!' she gasped in dismay. 'We'll have to turn back, your shirt has blown into the sea.'

'Tonight I'm not backtracking for anyone or anything,' he said, not bothering to glance round. He lifted his wrist to inspect the wide stainless steel watch. 'Five more minutes and we'll be there.'

For the first time Judith took note of her surroundings. The shore was a silver-gilt ribbon, fringed with the dark silhouettes of swaying palm trees. Occasional distant lights twinkled on fishing boats far out at sea, but the coastline was dark and uninhabited.

'We're going to Monkey Bay,' she smiled, as Linc
swung the wheel, steering them around a rocky
promontory. Once beyond the rocks they were alone.
The twinkling lights had vanished and there was no
other sign of life. Now it was just the two of them,
alone in the warmth of the tropical night where the
moon was their beacon, dappling black and silver
shadows on the crushed counterpane of the sea.

Linc's hand moved to her shoulder-blades where the
silver laces of her dress were caught into a bow. 'Help
me,' he murmured and her fingers meshed with his as
together they loosened the long silver ties. When they
were free, Linc slid the fine fabric down her hips and as
it fell to her feet she stepped out of it. Carelessly he
kicked it aside, concentrating only on her. Now just a
tiny pair of lace briefs adorned her.

'Honey,' he groaned, drinking in the sight of her
smooth body, the erotic swells, the shadowy clefts. He
cut the engine, leaving the cruiser to drift slowly in
towards the shore. His mouth was rough on hers, the
moustache and beard ravaging her skin as he kissed her.
Perspiration began to blend as he took her with him on
to the heady peaks of desire and, panting, she arched
herself against him as his hands stroked the silky
straining curves. As he fingered her taut nipples, she
whimpered out loud, lost in a daze of champagne and
need where everything was reduced to an elemental
level, where all that mattered was Linc—Linc kissing
her, fondling her, stroking her into ecstasy. Wild with
wanting, Judith ran her hands across his naked back,
sliding her fingers over the bulging mounds and hollows
of his muscles. Now he was caressing the soft
underslopes of her breasts, weighing them in his hands,
bending his head to needle the tight points with the tip
of his tongue.

There was a judder as the boat hit the beach. For a
moment Linc left her, stripping off the remainder of his

clothing and collecting towels from the cabin. After securing the boat, he held out his arms, carrying her through the warm shallows on to the sand. Wordlessly he pulled her down beside him on to the towels. 'Jude, my Jude,' he murmured.

Her heart was pounding like surf on a golden shore as she entered again into that domain of sensual pleasure of which Linc was the overlord, the supreme master. He possessed his own private supply of lightning, for every part of her tingled as he stroked, caressed, kissed her. Even the touch of his palm against hers was electric.

'I love you,' he said fiercely, dragging the tiny scrap of lace from her. 'You're mine, Jude, *mine!*'

He took her, shuddering as he came, flooding her with his love, and she flung back her head, her cries joining with his as together they hurled themselves into the reckless oblivion of desire.

All was peace. Judith lay in her husband's arms, drunk with warmth and tenderness which followed the intensity of his possession. Half awake, half asleep, she drifted on a high-flying cloud, feeling lightheaded and unreal. The bottle of champagne was empty, and now she murmured dreamily as he lifted the silken strands of her hair which were tousled across his chest, and kissed them. Lazily he began to arouse her all over again. This was the Linc she knew, and as her body responded to his, soft against his hardness, yielding to his masculinity, she told him again and again, 'I love you.'

CHAPTER EIGHT

'AAH!' With painful stealth Judith lifted a hand to her
head, tunnelling her fingers through the thick blonde
hair in an attempt to hold her skull together. 'Aah!' she
groaned again. She felt awful; every bone in her body
ached and her head was being mercilessly pounded by
some invisible sadistic drummer. Foggily she cast her
mind back, recalling the mix of drinks she had so rashly
consumed the previous evening, and wondered how she
could ever have been so cruel as to scorn people with
hangovers. It was true, you did feel like death!

Keeping very still she gingerly patted the bed beside
her—it was empty. Her fingers flailed in mid-air before
she located her watch and it took a few moments of
painful squinting before she could make sense of the
hands. One o'clock, she deciphered at last—lunchtime.
'Aah!' The prospect of food was nauseating. Every
movement was torture, even to close her eyes took
a supreme effort, but if she could fall asleep perhaps
she might wake up cured? Who was she kidding?
Hangovers like this didn't vanish into thin air. As she
lay there the realisation that the bungalow was deathly
quiet percolated through. Where were Linc and Magda?
Out on the patio maintaining a respectful silence? No,
Magda was incapable of keeping silent for long,
whatever the situation.

Time passed and eventually she forced herself to sit
upright. For a moment or two she crouched on the edge
of the bed before making a determined stumble towards
the bathroom. Two aspirins later she began the slow
process of pulling herself together. After a while she
made herself take a shower, and as the tepid water

streamed over her body she congratulated herself on her strength of will. By the time she had brushed her teeth and pulled on shorts and a matching top in lilac towelling, she felt better—still delicate, but better.

Judith padded out into the living-room in her bare feet and poked her head out on to the patio—it was deserted. Magda's room was also empty. Like a zombie she made for the kitchen and plugged in the percolator; wasn't black coffee supposed to sober you up? Though it wasn't as if she still felt tipsy, merely about to split into a thousand pieces. She was numbly sipping the hot liquid when there was a sound of a car on the drive, and tucking long strands of hair behind her ears, she walked carefully to the door. She blinked. Wayne was striding across the gravel.

'Hi, sugar,' he smiled. 'It's good to see you.'

Judith looked at him blankly. Why was he here? He seemed alarmingly like a man with a purpose as he marched in with a brisk stride, determination written all over his face.

'I'm not feeling too great. Would you mind keeping your voice down?' she pleaded.

He swung to confront her. 'What's the matter? What did he do to you?'

'What did who do to me?' she asked stupidly, sinking back down onto the sofa. 'Do you want coffee—or a beer?'

Impatiently Wayne shook his head. 'What did *Linc* do to you? I saw him forcing you away from the party last night and you never came back. Everyone was wondering what had happened.'

'He didn't actually force me,' she mused, then changed her mind. 'No, you're right, perhaps he did.'

'What's the score between you and Linc? Are you going to break up?'

She winced at his strident tone and struggled to gather her wits. Break up? Why should she and Linc break up when now everything was wonderful between them?

Wayne took her silence for affirmation. 'It's time for a showdown,' he declared, slamming a fist into his palm.

'A showdown?' She stared at him in bewilderment, wondering what on earth he was talking about.

'Linc needs to be told a few harsh facts,' he announced and she had never heard him sound so positive before. 'He must be made to realise he can't come back here and run our lives for us.'

'Don't you mean *ruin* your lives?' a dry voice inserted from the patio door.

Judith's head snapped round, hair flying, and then she moaned at the jarring impact. Linc was resting an indolent shoulder against the wall, totally relaxed, his thumbs tucked deep into the belt of his jeans. 'Have you been out?' she asked, wondering how long he had been stood there.

'Yes—jogging,' he told her, and she noticed how his sweat-damped tee shirt was clinging to his chest. 'I decided it would be a shame to let my present state of physical fitness deteriorate and become fat and flabby.'

'Huh! that's a long time off,' Wayne grunted, eyeing his cousin's lean frame.

'I hope so.' He folded his arms. 'I saw your car in the driveway. I'm surprised you didn't hide it away in the garage. Isn't that what usually happens when you visit my wife?'

Hot colour flooded Wayne's face. 'I don't know what you mean.'

'What are you talking about?' Judith interrupted. 'Can't we all be friends, like the old times?' She ignored Linc's air of disdain and smiled coaxingly. 'I would have thought after last night you'd be happy to . . .'

'Last night!' he sneered. 'Last night we'd both had

too much to drink, you especially. Last night didn't mean anything.'

She stared at him in horror. Had the heady combination of desire and champagne confused her? She had believed that all their troubles had disappeared and that now their marriage was secure, destined to be lifelong and full of love. Dispiritedly she tugged at a loose tendril of hair. Had it only been her imagination in the ecstasy of the night which had made it seem as though they were back together again spiritually as well as physically? A searing pain which had nothing to do with her hangover ripped across her chest, tearing the breath from her body. 'You can't mean that,' she gasped. 'I thought . . .'

'You thought what?' he demanded, his eyes flinty. 'Don't forget I can read body language as well as the next man. I saw you dancing with Wayne. Alcohol numbs the senses, and I dare say it didn't make much difference to you which of us you snared last night.' He shrugged. 'Still, I guess I expected this all along.'

'You're mad,' she said, holding a hand to her brow. 'Absolutely mad.'

He shrugged again, seemingly indifferent, and the gesture tore at her heart. So it wasn't Kee-Ann's plight which had kept him from her, there was something else, something far deeper. His love for her had gone, lost in the mists of the year apart, and the split could never be bridged.

'I confess I'm surprised that your friendship with Esther counts for so little. Cheating on her is like stabbing her in the back. I didn't expect that of you,' he drawled. 'But I imagine she'll be kept in the dark?' His brown eyes swung to Wayne. 'That's par for the course, isn't it? I presume Judith has been told you're happy to have an affair, but that it would take wild horses to drag you away from Esther, or is my wife the one who *will* drag you away?'

Eyes blazing, Judith leapt to her feet, galvanized into action by his naked scorn. 'There's nothing between Wayne and me! Okay, last night I was . . . I was flirting with him, but that was because I felt so broken up about you and Kee-Ann. Wayne and I have nothing to hide.'

'*Nothing*! From what I hear he's spent as much time with you over the past year as he has with Esther.'

'That's not true!' she flared, then her brow furrowed. She *had* seen Wayne most days. 'Yes, he came over a lot,' she admitted. 'But he was just being sociable, he was interested in my well-being.'

'It's your body he's interested in, lady.' Razor-sharp eyes sliced into Wayne. 'Isn't it?'

'Well . . . er . . . I think Judith is very nice, but. . . .' His flush deepened.

'Only nice?' Linc purred. 'Don't forget we're cousins, and as Magda would be quick to point out, we have the same genes. I know what turns me on and I'm damn sure I know what turns you on—my wife!'

'You have totally the wrong idea,' Judith snapped impatiently. 'If you imagine I would . . .'

'No, he hasn't,' Wayne cut in. 'Let's face it, Jude . . .'

'*Judith!*'

'Judith. If Linc had been away much longer things would have . . . well . . . developed between us.'

'*They certainly would not!*'

Wayne's mouth dropped open. 'Oh! But . . . but I thought you cared about me?'

'I did. I do. But purely on a platonic basis. If you must know I was working round to telling you to leave me alone and devote your time to Esther.' She looked down at her hands. 'As far as last night was concerned . . . I admit I was a bit tipsy.' She threw a withering look at Linc. 'And in a highly traumatic state.'

Linc's expression gave nothing away. He pushed his hands into his pockets and kept silent.

Wayne was staring dismally at his shoes. 'I guess I've made a fool of myself,' he muttered.

'Don't be hurt,' she said, walking to him and putting her hand on his arm. 'I'm very fond of you, and I really do appreciate everything you've done.'

At last Linc spoke, his eyes grave. 'I understand, Wayne,' he said slowly. 'It was a fraught situation. I don't blame you. I realise you wanted to comfort her, any man would.'

Wayne smiled weakly. 'Everything happened at once. I was going through a rough time at home, Esther was so goddamn wound up in the baby she never seemed to notice me, she didn't need me any more.'

'And Jude did?'

'I guess so, at least it felt like that. Everyone has told you how brave she was, but my word! it was all there beneath the surface. I wanted to reach out and make everything fine.'

'You helped me so much,' Judith said reassuringly. 'You kept Linc alive for me.' She looked across at her husband. 'Talking about you with Wayne kept my spirits high. He made you real, as though you were off on a business trip and due back soon. The only way I could believe you would return was to convince myself everything was partway normal, and discussing you with Wayne did just that.'

He gave a rueful laugh. 'Sounds like you were doing me a favour, cousin!'

'Perhaps so,' Wayne agreed, shamefaced. 'It was a difficult time all round. I guess I should have known Judith better.'

'You should!' she declared.

Linc shook his head wearily. 'Lord! the number of nights I used to lie awake hoping like hell you were looking after her, and yet hoping like hell you weren't.' He gave a loud sigh and flexed his shoulders as though a great weight had fallen from them. 'Thank heavens everything has turned out all right.'

'You should have had more trust,' Judith chided as his arm tightened around her waist, then her eyes grew troubled. 'But so should I.'

'In a situation like the one we've been through it's not only a matter of trust,' he replied, frowning. 'To be honest, I couldn't have found it in my heart to blame you if something had happened. I know how low I felt at times, how desperate I was for a kind word, a friendly smile, a shoulder to cry on. It's only when you're deprived of affection that you realise how greedy you are for it. It's a staple of life, we all need someone to snuggle up to when things are hard.'

'I guess you're right,' Wayne said with a grin. 'I'd better go home now and snuggle up to Esther. Who knows, she might discover she likes big boys as well as little ones!'

Everyone laughed.

'We're going to discuss our plans for the future,' Linc told him as they walked towards the front door. 'I'll let you know as soon as we reach a decision. It's unfair to keep you dangling.'

Wayne hesitated on the porch. 'Whatever happens, Esther and I will be staying on in Penang. We discussed the possibility of your moving on and she thinks it's best if we stay and consolidate.' He raised a brow. 'Once you prise her away from the baby talk she's got some shrewd ideas.'

'Women are full of surprises,' Linc chuckled, smiling down at Judith with warm brown eyes.

She dug her fingernails into the gap of bare brown skin between his tee shirt and jeans. 'It's men who are too stupid to read the signs properly!'

He wriggled. 'Ouch! perhaps you're right.'

She prodded again.

'Okay, you *are* right.'

'I'm pleased you're still on good terms,' Judith said as Wayne drove away. 'He was very kind.'

'I don't doubt it, but he's no angel,' Linc pronounced, sitting beside her on the sofa and thrusting a hairy arm around her shoulders. 'Mind you, he specialises in married women, women who are unlikely to demand a commitment. There's something Freudian there! Wayne strays, but always ends up paddling in shallow water. He'd probably have shot back to Esther if you had welcomed his attentions!' His grin faded. 'But then, perhaps not.'

Judith nestled against his chest. 'I would never have become involved with him,' she insisted.

'I know that now, but I've had some harrowing moments. Jeez! the thought of you and Wayne together has haunted me all week,' he confessed, burying his face in her hair. 'I was so happy when we first met again, but then when you began to apologise for something and Wayne walked in. . . . Well, I put two and two together and made far too many. Emotionally I was in pretty poor shape. I'd been out of touch for so long that I didn't know what to believe; I wavered backwards and forwards, worrying myself sick.'

'And I thought you didn't care any more,' she murmured, running her fingertips across the rich growth of beard. 'You were so distracted, I imagined Kee-Ann was continually on your mind.'

'No, honey, it was you. I did feel responsible for her, but that's not what kept me awake nights. I was worried sick that you wanted to end our marriage, and everything seemed to confirm my suspicions. When you told me you didn't want a child I saw it as proof you had decided our relationship was shaky, to say the least!' He solemnly rubbed his brow against hers. 'I don't know how I survived. It was the final blow when you blithely announced you had no wish to go to the States with me.'

'You rushed me, Linc. You had life all arranged without consulting me. I . . . I rebelled.'

'And how! I couldn't get the hang of you. I know we'd had the odd quarrel in the past, but suddenly you were so godawful independent. It was difficult to assimilate all the facts. Half the trouble was that while I was held hostage I'd had too much time to think. I had this scenario of you in my head—pale and wan, dressed in grey lace, pining for me, drifting helplessly through the days. When I arrived home and discovered that you were totally controlled and running a flourishing business. . . .' He shook his head in bewilderment. 'To be honest, your success with the antiques scared the pants off me. I felt so insecure.'

Judith's brows lifted. '*You*—insecure!'

'I'm only human, and perhaps, until now, I have tended to be. . . .' He gave the ghost of a chuckle, 'patronising where the female sex are concerned. I suppose, deep down, I've always presumed I knew best. Don't forget I was programmed at thirteen, so I've had years of practice. Before my father died we had long talks, and he was insistent I should take over his place in the house. He was a lot older than Magda and he treated her like a foolish child.'

'That wouldn't have been difficult!'

'It wasn't. He instilled into me that when he had gone it was my duty to look after her. I was at a very impressionable age, so when he died I was damned eager to do all I could for my mother, and Megda being Magda, she revelled in it.'

'And the habit was formed.'

'Yes, and it spilled over on to all my relationships with women, including you.'

'Which is why you were so delighted when I drove into the drain!'

The slashes in his cheeks dimpled uncontrollably. 'It was kind of amusing.'

'But untypical,' she slanted.

'I agree. It was an isolated incident, but at the time it put you on a level with Magda.'

'Thank you!'

He spread a hand in an easy gesture. 'But don't you see, I could deal with that. It made me feel like big daddy. I guess it's a role I've unconsciously played ever since my father died. Certainly all my dealings with Magda have been on that basis. Kee-Ann, too, once she accepted I wasn't prepared to lay her. Everyone has always said "Good old Linc, he'll take charge", so I have.' His grin was self-mocking. 'You're the first woman to buck the system. It was one helluva blow to my ego when I discovered you had coped perfectly well without me.'

'Not that well, darling,' she told him, her face clouding. 'I lost the baby because my nerves were in shreds. I was bottling everything up. I managed to get through the days in one piece, but night after night I sobbed myself to sleep.'

Linc stroked her hair. 'It's all right now.'

'But is it?' she fretted. 'Like it or not, the past year has changed us. Our relationship will never be the same again.'

'It'll be better,' he said firmly. 'Before, we hadn't gotten around to being completely honest, we were both acting out roles, but now we've been given a fresh start.'

'Do you really want to move to San Francisco?' she probed.

Linc rubbed his jaw reflectively. 'Yes, I do. Setting up an operation in the States makes far more sense from a commercial viewpoint. Penang is tiny; all we need is for another helicopter line to set up an operation and we'd be in dead trouble, the market isn't broad enough to support two. We've almost reached the limit as far as expansion goes here anyway, and if we're to grow it must be into other Asian countries, and that will involve the usual restrictions on foreigners.'

'You'd rather be based in the States where the sky's the limit?' she asked, grinning at the unconscious pun.

He grinned back. 'Yes, but. . . .'

'But what?'

'But I'm hesitant of making the decisions for us again.' He gave her a long hard look. 'From a business angle a move makes sense, but from the personal angle . . . well, I just don't know.'

'I don't want to wear the trousers, Linc.'

'Why not? You have the cutest backside in the business,' he teased.

'Don't evade the issue!'

'No, ma'am.' He bent his head to kiss her, then ran the tip of his tongue slowly across her lower lip. 'Come to bed, let me make love to you.'

'That's evasion,' she protested, wondering where her hangover had gone, for now happiness was sparkling in her veins.

'Are you afraid you might get pregnant? It's too late to start worrying now, honey. Ten to one it's happened already. You were real abandoned last night.'

'*I* was abandoned!'

He grinned. 'You sure were.'

'I thought you said last night didn't mean anything.'

'I'm a liar. Hell, every time I touch you I'm telling you I love you.' A shadow crossed his eyes. 'If you really are serious about not starting a family yet, then I'm prepared to wait until next week when you can get fixed up. I can't say I'll like it, but I will wait.'

'You just said it was too late to start worrying!'

His mouth crooked. 'Well, I don't know if we're likely to be so productive second time around.'

'I think we should give it a try.'

'You do?'

'I do. Suddenly the prospect of us having a baby

seems far more exciting than running an antique business.'

'I don't think you should rush into this. . . .' Linc began, then pulled a face as there came the sound of a car outside and Magda's high-pitched shout of farewell.

'That Mr Jeyaretnam's real cute,' she declared, sweeping into the bungalow in a floral kaftan. 'He's invited me to stay with him in Calcutta. I dare say he owns a palace there.'

'How nice.' Linc reluctantly separated himself from Judith.

'But I'm not sure if I should go, what do you think? Is it very foreign?'

'Everywhere's foreign apart from L.A.,' he drawled. 'And I think you should make up your own mind.'

She fingered the hoop of her earring. 'Should I? Yes, I suppose I should.'

'I'm sorry I wasn't up earlier,' Judith said apologetically. 'I had a hangover.'

'But you're fine now?' her mother-in-law enquired, then, without waiting for a reply, continued, 'I've had a great morning. I joined Mr Jeyaretnam at the poolside for brunch. We were discussing the party last night. Wasn't it a wonderful surprise for you both!'

'It was lovely,' Judith agreed.

'Thanks very much,' Linc joined in, though his smile seemed a little forced.

Magda preened smugly for a moment or two, then she frowned. 'I do wish you would hurry up and shave off that awful beard, Lincoln. It looks so ... so unAmerican!'

He ran a large hand across his jaw. 'And I thought I was the epitome of one of your Russian princes!'

'Well, now that you mention it. . . .' she began, then her voice petered out as she realised he could be teasing. She smoothed her skirt down over her hips and said tartly, 'There's a photograph of you in the newspaper, but nobody will recognise you with that dreadful beard.'

'Let me have a look.' Judith pounced on the newspaper and leafed rapidly through the pages until she came to the article. There was a large photograph of Linc standing in the garden. 'I think you look very dashing,' she declared and was rewarded with a broad smile.

'It's the Lincoln Cassidy Mark Two,' he grinned. 'The improved model.'

'And what was wrong with the old one?' Magda asked sharply.

'Well. . . .' Judith caught her lower lip between her teeth, blue eyes shining.

'He had a tendency to run everyone's lives for them,' Linc said. 'Especially yours, Mother, but it's coming to an end. As a final gesture I shall ring the airport and confirm your ticket for tomorrow. After that you're on your own.'

'On my own?' Magda said uncertainly. 'Ticket for tomorrow? But I don't leave for at least three more days and actually I was thinking. . . .'

'You leave tomorrow,' he told her. 'You've enjoyed a good holiday, but now you must show some consideration and allow Jude and me time alone together in our own home. And in future you can quit sending me frantic telegrams and phoning in the middle of the night, because I'll come and see you when *I* want to come, and not when you're bored or you need the roof fixing.'

'Lincoln! How can you treat your own mother like this?' Magda asked, fluttering her lashes in agitation, a habit Judith found rather comical.

'Easily,' he retorted. 'For the past twenty-odd years I've been at your beck and call, always giving, never taking, and I reckon I deserve a break. You're relatively young, you're healthy and you have money in the bank.

There's no reason at all why I should continue to run round in circles.' He grinned at Judith. 'I have enough on my plate dealing with this wife of mine.'

'Then I shall marry Cy,' Magda announced, bosom heaving.

Linc and Judith shared a look of astonishment.

'Does he want to marry you?' Judith asked cautiously.

'Of course! Why do you imagine he's been telephoning me so often?'

'And he's proposed?'

'Cy's always proposing,' she snapped. 'And now I have no alternative but to accept his proposal. A woman like me needs a man to look after her. In any case, perhaps it's time I settled down.' She swept regally to her feet. 'I shall start my packing now, then I shall drive along to the hotel and say goodbye to Mr Jeyaretnam. Kindly tell the airport I require an aisle seat in the "no smoking" section, where I can see the film. Oh, and towards the front of the plane.' She flounced away, waggling her hips.

Linc gave a long low whistle. 'I repeat, women sure are full of surprises. I'd never have believed I could have gotten Magda off my back so easily.'

'You never tried before,' Judith pointed out.

'True, but I imagined she was helpless.'

'Like me?'

'I slotted you in the same pigeonhole, but boy! did I miscalculate.' He ran his fingers through his hair. 'It amazes me how we ever managed to get through our first year of married life so smoothly.'

'Everything was new, Linc, so I had to depend on you. There were so many adjustments to be made— living in a strange country, setting up home.' Her eyes sparkled. 'Getting used to making love to a foreigner!'

'Don't tell me they do it differently in England!' he chuckled.

'They do it more often,' she retorted, the corner of her mouth lifting. 'My experience is that big butch Californians cut out sex for twelve months at a time.'

'It's all the surfing, it saps the strength,' he said, deadpan.

'You surfed a lot in the jungle?'

'Well . . . no.'

'So you're feeling quite strong?'

He stroked his chin with his fingers. 'I guess I could rise to the occasion if necessary. Shall we go to bed and find out?'

Magda poked her head out of the bedroom door. 'Have you telephoned the airport yet, Lincoln?'

'Goddammit!'

'There's no call to swear,' she said snootily.

'I'll do it now,' he promised, rising to his feet, and Magda disappeared again.

'While you're on the phone ask about flights to San Francisco,' Judith said.

He narrowed his eyes. 'Why?'

'Because if we're intending to live there we'd better fly over and reconnoitre.'

'*Are* we intending to live there?'

'I am,' she declared.

Linc shrugged broad shoulders. 'And you know me, always ready to fall in with someone else's ideas.'

'You mean you're easily led?'

'Absolutely.'

She smiled at him. 'I bet you're the kind of guy who lets women have their way with him?'

Putting his arms around her waist, he pulled her close. 'Wom*a*n,' he corrected. 'But that's me, never been known to resist. I'm just an antique shop owner's plaything.' He ran a large hand over her rear end. 'And I do like the way you kind of curve out of your shorts.'

Judith kissed his cheek. 'Telephone first, Mr Cassidy!'

'Yes, ma'am.' He lifted the receiver and then put it down. 'Are you sure about moving back to the States?' he asked, suddenly serious. 'If you prefer to stay on in Penang we can postpone a move.'

'I'm quite sure,' she said firmly. 'I've been thinking things over and I agree now is the best time for us to make a move. I'll be sorry to part with Mandarin Antiques, but I have some excellent contacts in South-East Asia, so if I open another shop. . . .'

'When.'

'When I open another shop in San Francisco, I shall be starting off with a firm trading base. However, as now also seems an ideal time to start a family, if I've not already started, perhaps I shall put the idea of a shop on ice for a year or two.'

Linc frowned. 'But you're giving way all along the line.'

'I'm not, darling, I'm seeing sense. I needed some kind of fulfilment over the past year and Mandarin Antiques provided it, but it was only a replacement—a replacement for you and the baby I lost.' She lifted the receiver and handed it to him. 'But now we have a second chance. We might be two slightly different people, but one thing has remained the same.'

'Our love,' he murmured against her lips. 'That has always been constant.'

The helicopter swooped down across the nodding topknots of the palm trees towards the silver-white beach. Linc concentrated on a smooth landing, checking the instruments, positioning the small craft in exactly the right place above the sand. Beside him, strapped into her safety belt, Judith watched. His love of flying shone in his eyes as he whistled beneath his breath, searching for just the right position, ears attuned to the noise of the engine. When he was satisfied that the revs were correct for their descent he lined up the chopper, co-ordinating with precision, taking account of the soft breeze buffeting against the bubble of the aircraft. Easing off the throttle, he adjusted the pitch of the blades for a soft landing. The machine settled comfortably on the hard sand, and when he had completed the shutdown drill, he turned to her. 'Monkey Bay, as requested, ma'am. Your final visit, at least for the time being.'

She smiled.

'Stay where you are,' he instructed. 'I'll come and help you.'

Judith hid a fond grin in his direction as she unbuckled the safety belt. 'I'm not an invalid,' she protested as he came round to her side of the chopper and lifted her out.

'I have to look after you,' he smiled, his eyes warm and soft upon her. 'And that baby of ours.'

Together they walked down the sand towards the turquoise-blue shallows where tiny white-crested waves lapped at the shore.

'No regrets?' he asked, slipping an arm around her shoulders.

'I shall miss Penang, but no, no real regrets,' she admitted. 'I imagined it would be painful to sell Mandarin Antiques, but it wasn't.' She glanced down fondly at the still flat stomach. 'Having the baby to consider suddenly made the shop take second place.'

Linc gave a chuckle of delight. 'You've confounded Esther again, she's convinced you hold the key to instant conception!'

'It takes two to tango,' she glinted.

'And, honey, I just love the rhythm.'

She flashed him a teasing glance. 'Is that why you've brought me here today?'

'However could you think such a thing?' he demanded, eyes wide and innocent. 'I'm merely taking you on a whistle-stop tour of the island before we leave tomorrow.'

'So it's five minutes here and then we fly off to one of the tourist spots?'

The slashes in his cheeks deepened below the beard. 'Well,' he said slowly. 'Purely by chance I happen to have with me a bottle of wine and some chicken drumsticks and salad. I don't suppose you fancy staying here for lunch?'

'But it's only ten o'clock,' she protested, laughing.

'We could make it a long lunch,' he murmured into her hair. 'After all, we have so much to discuss.'

'Like what?'

'Like names for the baby, and whether I love you more than you love me, and how wonderful your skin tastes in the sunshine, and. . . .'

'And why you just happen to possess the broadest shoulders,' she continued, wrapping her arms around his neck. 'And how the hair on your chest curls when it's damp, and why I can't live without you.'

He smiled, putting a long finger across her lips. 'We'll save the discussion for lunchtime, right? But now . . . Jude, hey Jude, I love you!'

A WORD ABOUT THE AUTHOR

Although her first novel wasn't penned until she was nearly forty, Elizabeth Oldfield actually began writing professionally when she was a teenager. She had enrolled in a writing course taught by mail. As guaranteed, the course more than paid for itself with the money she subsequently earned from sales of her writing to magazines and newspapers—but at that stage of her life, writing was really only a hobby. Soon other types of work outside the home and family life took her away from dreams of living by her pen.

After a number of years of marriage, her husband, a mining engineer, was posted to Singapore for a five-year spell. Here Elizabeth enjoyed not only exciting leisure activities—tennis, handicrafts, entertaining fascinating visitors from all over the globe—but also the opportunity to absorb as much as possible about a culture as varied as it was exotic. And having more time on her hands, she resumed her writing—once again finding success at articles, interviews and humorous pieces.

But she had a larger goal: to write a book. Romance novels caught her eye. By the time she left Singapore, she had completed two novels and eventually saw both published—sending her on her way as a romance novelist. Now she works four days a week on her books, spending the rest of her time in various activities, including, whenever possible, hours spent with her family.